Notes / E

TABLE OF CONTENTS

We sigh, stretch, and push myself away from my laptop. I allow the chair spin for prior to lazily dragging my foot to stop it. I was indeed working on a story that is new. One about Christmas, and the horrors it includes. It was pretty cheesy, and all sorts of the basic ideas felt recycled. Psycho elves, murderous Santas, hungry reindeer, you understand the drill. We desire to surrender, but I have abandoned enough tasks. My pet, Sam, rubs against my feet and purrs. He could be selected by me up and he lays on my lap for one minute. Sometimes, I don't mind this life. I stay by myself and nobody bothers me personally. It's moments like this that I feel guiltiest for wanting more. I understand I've got nothing going on. If I passed away now in my own seat, nobody would notice. I look at the full time, and realize it's previous midnight already. I pull myself out of my seat and flop face-first on my sleep. We rearrange my covers and close my eyes. Right we swear we hear tiny footsteps, a giggle, and the band of a bell when I drift off.

My eyes snap open. I prop myself up on my elbows and check my clock. It's only 2 have always been. I watch out the window to discover snow. Day it's Christmas. I can't believe We forgot. The snow is dropping so perfectly; it almost feels like my story. I hear that damn bell again, and turn towards my door.

We cautiously walk out of my room and turn my hallway light on. I quietly make my way downstairs and switch on all the lights in my own house. Nobody's here. Something special is noticed by me under my tree. It's a medium-sized box, covered with dark paper that is red. I don't keep in mind putting it there.

I kneel down as I approach the box. I carefully tear the paper off. The container is red, too. The box is opened by me and instantly vomit. My pet is inside it, their formerly gray and black body that is striped red. An eyeball has fallen out of its socket. His entrails were accustomed tie their paws together. Mutilated beyond recognition, the way in which is only know it's him is because of his dark blue collar sitting together with his matted fur. I vomit again and start crying. I pick up his collar. His name happens to be crossed out.

We run backup to my room and slam the door. On my wall surface, 'Merry Christmas' has been written on my walls, in what appears like blood. I run to my computer to search for internet connectivity. My phone was kept downstairs, so that is away from issue. My computer turns in, and there, displayed on the screen, is my story. I read it starts sounding familiar through it, and. The type that is main pet gets savagely slaughtered, after which the key character must fight for her life against Christmas gone wrong.

We know very well what will happen next, and I'm terrified. Every cliché into the written guide is approximately to become alive. Everything that I laugh at in my stories is about to kill me. We do a check that is quick of cabinet and under my bed before plopping myself down in front of the home. I start crying once more, but shut up when I hear something prancing on the rooftop, and appropriate on cue, out jumps good Santa that is old Claus. The reindeer are here.

I scramble to my feet and start barricading my door. I hear slow, heavy steps coming up my stairs. I open my window and put my fire ladder out. I run to my backpack, empty it out, and put my laptop inside it. We require to keep monitoring of my enemies. Suddenly, I'm determined to survive. I pull my hair that is tangled into ponytail, slip-on shoes, and put on my jacket. Something starts beating on my door.

I swing my leg over the windowsill and down start climbing. My door splinters open and two elves riding a reindeer burst through. I consider jumping, but I'm on the ground that is second. I climb faster, but only get about halfway down before an elf sometimes appears by me peek out the window. He looks like one thing you would see in a Christmas movie. He's got pink, rosy cheeks and shiny hair that is black. He smiles cruelly and pulls out a knife to cut my rope. He smiles and waves as I fall.

In the beginning, I can't breathe. I desperately gasp before finally getting a breath that is short. Something lands which are cold my face. Personally I think around me. We landed on snowfall. It's snowing! The wind picks up. It's want it started just for me! We start laughing. My hysterical laughter rings through the yard. We wave my arms around me, making this snow angel that is strange.

I stand straight back up, brushing off my garments, and bump my backpack. My laptop! I landed right on top of it! We can't think I forgot about any of it!

We shrug my bag off and unzip it. My computer is in 2 pieces. I don't know what direction to go next. I can't remember what goes on next. How will I endure?

"No," I say to myself. "I will never be beaten by a children's legend and furries!" I decide to go in through the door that is back due to the fact my fence is too tall to climb up. I have to have left it an unlocked the night that is last because it swings open with ease. I don't trust this, but I'm out of choices and time.

A horrifying scene greets me upon entry. The walls are streaked with blood. It looks fresh. The stove has a pot that is big on it. I just take a knife from the block and approach it slowly. We turn fully off the peek and gas inside. In it, there's a bright Santa that is red hat. Why would he boil their own cap? Nothing they are doing makes feeling. That isn't how the whole story goes. I broke the copy that is only of tale, so it should stop! Appropriate? Let's say they are free since they aren't bound to the story? If they are free, only one thing shall distinguish my character from me. My character shall have survived. I grip the knife tighter and continue through the kitchen.

I make my way through the living room and back to the Christmas tree. The" that is"present gone, nevertheless the memory and bloodstains aren't. We hear bells again. I whip around violently and face the chimney. I hear someone softly chanting "ho, ho, ho" over and over. I do want to scream and cover my ears, do anything to stop it. It's not jolly or happy. Simply a mantra that is monotonous.

I wish to light a fire under his ass, but the logs have actually been eliminated. Rather, We run back upstairs, knowing they're all watching me, chasing me. I'm not just paranoid. They can be heard by me whispering, laughing at me. Following me. I slide under my sleep. My elbow hits something and personally i think a sharp, stabbing pain. The secret is pulled by me object out of my arm and examine it. It's an item of wood. It's painted midnight blue, with silver and stars which are gold. It's a right element of my door. My home has been destroyed and is scattered around my room. We have no other cover.

Heavy, deliberate footsteps ascend my staircase, followed by light, fast ones. The people being heavy be Santa additionally the light ones must function as the elves. His reindeer are gone. Shiny boots that are black colored within my door and I also hold my breath. They slowly meander over to my bed and stand in front of it.

I remember that whenever I happened to be little, I became scared of Santa. I refused to sit on their lap. Or write letters. Or recognize Christmas. It was just another day for me personally. I'm not sure why I was so scared of Santa back then, but I understand why I'm scared now. In all honesty, I feel the right is had by me to be petrified of Santa if I survive this.

Who am I kidding? There's no real way i stand a chance. You will find no superheroes to save me. No mother to sit she could just get one goddamn picture with me so.

My name is Aubrey Green. I have always been 24 yrs . old. Last was my birthday celebration week. We have red hair that is frizzy freckles. I code for a full time income. I never met my neighbors. I haven't spoken to my mother in very nearly a and I haven't seen my dad since I have was 10 year. I was bullied a lot as a youngster and have scars being self-harm. I'm still putting on my pajamas, a pink and tank that is black colored, black shorts, and pink knee-high socks that look like cats.

I hear sirens.

In hours that are few my mother will get a call. She'll fall to her knees and cry, but she'll be okay in time. The sirens are closer, but not close enough. Someone cared about me enough to call for help. The situation that is just, quickly, none of this will matter, because, in a few seconds, I will be dead.

A CHRISTMAS DAY SANTA'S MAGIC

The night of Christmas Eve 2008 is a blur, according to how medication that is much am given that day. The nurses can be avoided by me for a couple of hours, yet not too long. I suppose you've learned about me in the documents or on your own favorite killer show that is serial. No, I was never convicted. Just what the news claimed had been all lies anyway. No one knew what happened that except me personally – which is why the police blamed me personally night. My title is Max and my name is all we carry now. You've probably heard of ghost towns across the U.S. My town is one of these. Based in the foggy mountains of Oregon, people haven't heard about the town "Asher." It was the type of town where individuals never left, and they always returned if they did. Things and individuals always had a habit of coming back. Bad memories, sadness, pain, and grief constantly stuck around. Festering at right before one tried to go to bed, piling on itself, growing deeper in the dirt evening. There are woodlands, but perhaps not as many woods we would have as you'd think. Green doesn't grow in this town. The dirt won't let it.

No matter how sage that is much burned, it couldn't clean this place. This town was haunted, but perhaps, the social people were first. I don't consider myself haunted, I just think I happened to be born wrong. Me personally that I wasn't like other babies when I was brought into this world, my mother told. I'd a face that is solemn-looking dark eyes. She also said that I declined to cry. I still can't cry. My eyes won't tears that are produce. It is said by the doctors's a problem. Even if my grandmother died, I never cried. Or when my mom would scream I never flinched at me. Or when my dog got struck by a car.

Absolutely Nothing.

I didn't feel things like other kids or people. I don't feel at all.

I knew something was incorrect when I accidentally cut half my finger off and I never screamed when I was six. There clearly was something within me that isn't in other folks. I guess it was destiny for the events that took place. Some sort of fated magic.

Whenever my mother got drunk, I would personally be told by her that I happened to be a stone boy and that all stone boys went to hell. She was bi-polar when she wanted to be. Me, she loved me, but whenever she despised the very fact that she had a kid, she hated me personally when she loved. There was never an in-between.

My father was too busy nothing that is pretending wrong, with his mind in the clouds of denial, he constantly knew how to make himself feel better. All he had to away do was look or leave the house. Too bad I couldn't reside in those clouds with him. Rather, I had been always by myself, sitting in silence during the kitchen table, staring out the window in the chair that is back of car, waiting for some better day to come, but better times never arrived.

2008 was a of numerous things for me personally year. We had started grade that is 8th had been finally 12 months from senior school. My sound got significantly deeper and life seemed want it had possibilities, until my parents separated. The separation made my home life worst. My mother drank more and my father never came home. The teachers blamed me for not attention that is spending but what they didn't understand was that I hadn't eaten in 2 days. The school bully would make fun of my ribs and call me names. He was called by us Dan the Giant. At almost 6 legs at thirteen years old, he had been monstrous. The person that is only than him ended up being his father. His dad was taller than him and viler. Perhaps the trained teachers were scared. Dan had dyslexia too, but he wasn't that bright, in the first place. Any kid that corrected or mentioned him got the beating. Any kid that existed, to be honest, got a beating. Dan stuck gum in my hair the before Winter Break friday. The teacher had to cut chunks of my brown strands that are curly get it away. My dad blamed me saying I deserved it because we refused to stick up for myself. How the hell ended up being I supposed to stick up to a behemoth that is six-foot? They would all get theirs, I promised myself. One day – they would have it. This city that is whole.

The teacher had us all do an exercise. It was called by her Santa's Magic. We'd to write a letter to Santa asking just what we wanted many. The other young ones laughed. All of us knew Santa Claus wasn't real. For a quick moment, I believed, because I had nothing else to have confidence in. I asked Santa for something important. Something I've wanted for a while that is long. Something just Santa could offer me.

* * * * * *

A can was being made by me of soup when my mother stumbled through the kitchen, knocking the bowl out of my hand. "Pick it up!" she yelled. Perhaps not wanting to get hit, some towels were found by me and soaked up the liquid. My dad looked down at me from the living room without saying a word. Instead, he took his coat and left. God, I hated my parents. They were pieces of cow crap and it was known by them. The town that is whole who my mom had been by the bars she'd frequent and lose her clothing in. Dan the Giant when told the class that my mother was nothing but a whore that is no-good my father a loser mechanic. Which was the i punched Dan day. Of course, he punched right back and harder. Neither of us got in trouble. The principal did want to get n't involved. That was the simple thing with the city of Asher. No one desired conflict, yet there ended up being always conflict. No one wanted to get involved, yet everyone usually was.

We put the towels that are soaked-up the basement and went along to mop the floor. I was upset because that was the might that is last of. No one went food shopping anymore and whenever something did usually pop up someone took it and hid it. We scrambled through the cabinets for other things i possibly could find. There was nothing. I teared up, my stomach growling, and a glass had been drunk by me of water to appease the pain sensation. My mother sat into the corner associated with kitchen with her bottle, laughing.

"Where did your father get?" She asked, stuttering over her words.

"I don't know," I responded.

"One i'm going to leave this earth and never come back day. Then what are you all going to do?" She laughed again. "You're exactly like your dad. Small, weak, and pitiful. I did son't want you, but I was made by him help keep you," she chided. Day"we never wanted kids, but there you're one. A mistake."

"Stop," I muttered under my breath.

"Or what?" my mother replied, vicious as ever.

My father came back through the door. He took one check my mother and went upstairs to his space.

"The young ones within the town state you're a whore," I screamed.

My mother got up from the bottom as quickly as she fell back over.

"what the hell did you call me? just"

"My friends say you're nothing but a dirty whore!"

My mom reached into the drawer and grabbed a blade.

"You piece of shit. How dare you dare call me that. How will you think I pay for this place? Your father, who hasn't had a functional work in months? Your weak and father that is useless. Weak and useless! And also you understand what? You're similar to him!" She screamed. My mother took another swing at the bottle then at me.

"Just get out! Get out! Escape my house! GET OUT!" she screamed.

I grabbed my backpack and went away, not looking back. I just ran, not knowing where I was going. I ran knowing that We couldn't go back. Tears flowed down my eyes and my chest felt enjoy it would definitely drop my ass out. I need to have pissed myself because my jeans were wet. We went through the roads, at night academic school, past the city, into the woods. The sun had already gone down and also the night took over producing an path that is eerie the outskirts of town. I did care that is n't. I ran through the trees, going off the trail, finally stopping once I had no fresh air left in my own lungs. My legs collapsed and I sat against a tree.

The wind blew against my face and for the time that is first that whole run, we realized I was utterly alone. Not simply in these woods. No family had been had by me personally. No friends had been had by me. No one was had by me personally. I desired never to occur anymore. For a brief moment, I wondered exactly what it would were prefer to die. To not be me. Until something shuffled amongst the leaves. I got up and looked out to the darkness. We couldn't see anything. We tried to inform myself until I heard the shuffling once more that it had been nothing. It had been Oregon, so perhaps it absolutely was a bear or an animal moving about. The shuffling had been heavy. Shuffling and steps being taken by one thing big and bigger than me. We tiptoed in the dark to try and find the trail. I was mortified. Without any flashlight or even the moon to aid, we was blind. I heard the shuffling again, except closer.

My heart was like an engine failing. I really couldn't breathe. We kept walking, comprehending that whatever the hell was shuffling for the reason that darkness, knows I happened to be here. It was when I felt a tactile hand on my shoulder that We started initially to run. I didn't know if We going deeper to the woodland, but We went if We ended up being going the right way or. Just as much I would gladly go back to my crazy mother than maintain the woods with one thing I couldn't see as we hated my moms and dads. Luckily for us, I became going the way that is right I heard an automobile drive by. It was produced by me personally straight back to the road, but i really could nevertheless feel whatever it was in that timber, behind me. I waved at the engine car driving, screaming for help. A rock had been taken by me and tossed it during the car. It smashed a window. The vehicle reversed and stopped.

"Help me personally!" I screamed. The car pulled over and a guy wearing a plaid that is red with a long grimy beard got out of the vehicle.

"Help!" I yelled.

"What the fuck would you think you're doing, you little shit?!" he screamed, examining their automobile.

"There's something after me personally!" I yelled.

"I don't give a fuck. Look what you did, you little shit."

"There's someone out here following me. Please!" I pleaded.

"You better hope your moms and dads will pay with this or I'll chop your balls off as payment!" he screamed.

The grimy man that is bearded me personally by my neck and slammed me against the car.

"Or maybe I should do it now," he said. His breath smelled like beer and cheese that is rotten. He had been missing a tooth in the side that is left of mouth. I turned away, terrified.

Me, I fell to the bottom before he could strike. Something dragged the bearded, grimy man away from me.

"Kid, get the weapon in my car!" he yelled at me, blood coming from his nose.

We went into his truck and discovered a revolver under the seat. I possibly could hear something attacking the person that is bearded. The thing from the forests. The tearing could possibly be heard by me personally of flesh and the breaking of his bones. I grabbed the device that is man's had fallen on a lawn and put it on flashlight mode. The man ended up being dragged into the woods, screaming, leaving a bloodstain on the road behind. I screamed and went in to the motor car, locking the doors. I didn't understand how to drive a motor vehicle, but I figured it out. We put my base regarding the brakes and out of the gear in drive. Despite the fact that I put my foot regarding the gas, the vehicle wouldn't go. Whatever creature took that man, returned, this right time, for me. It absolutely was keeping the motor car through the back. I got out and started running straight back through the dark. I attempted to call 911 on the dude's cell-phone, but something knocked it out of my hand, smashing it to the ground.

We stopped, feeling the creature circling me. I prepared myself to be torn apart like the grimy man that is bearded. Rather, I felt a breath that is stale my throat. We turned around, not anything that is seeing. I knew it would be any brief moment before it killed me. I closed my eyes and waited. My hand raised on its own. Whatever this creature was, held my hand and grasped it, holding it. I shakily lifted the light from the cell-phone to its face. It absolutely was ugly with white pale and skin that is scaly. Its lips ended up being oversized with teeth that protruded from the bloodied mouth. A lengthy tongue that is slippery stuck on the way a snake's tongue feels the environment. It absolutely was tall, and had black coal eyes that provided a stare that is merciless.

"What are you?" I asked.

The eyes that are cold into mine, but it gave no response.

"Th… th… thank you," we muttered.

An ice had been felt by me droplet on my nose. It started to snow. I didn't know what this thing ended up being, but it decided it Creature that I would phone.

Creature cried to the night. Its shrieks echoed into the atmosphere. I happened to be still scared, but one thing felt safe with it. I happened to be saved because of it from that guy.

"Are you alone, too?" We asked.

It shook its mind. Whatever Creature was, I was understood because of it.

The creature took one appearance that is last me and ran into the woods, disappearing to the woods.

We ran house and away from just what would be a crime scene that is future. I was terrified, confused, but also curious. I opened my home that is front quietly hoping that no body was awake and tiptoed to my bed room.

* * * * * *

The morning that is next the entire city was talking of bears, thieves, or wild animals that must took Burton John -A.K. A – The grimy man that is bearded. That was his name. Only I knew just what happened to Burton and he had been certainly dead. I guessed Creature took the physical body and finished it off elsewhere. My mother left me alone the day that is next perhaps out of guilt. My father never asked me just how I was. I quickly got went and dressed off to school.

Night i didn't notice the dirt within my hair leftover from last. Dan the Giant made jokes to the course about how exactly poor my family had been that we had been all dirty people that we couldn't pay for water and. We ignored him, but he just wouldn't stop. For an entire 30 moments, he kept going, unable to manage himself. The teacher sat at her computer drinking her coffee, living in her clouds of denial, and nothing that is pretending wrong.

Then the thought came to me.

How interesting would it be to own Creature eat Dan?

It ended up being murder, I quickly recognized, and I wasn't a murderer. Dan kept going for the rest of the class period. Something changed in me. I realized Dan didn't deserve mercy. He deserved to get eaten. He was a bit of shit and he would eventually grow around be a shit adult. People like him never grew out of their shit-ness. Teenagers like Dan either became men that are violent preyed in bars or violent cops that preyed on civilians.

He would be missed by no body.

Remembering the gum in my hair and I also knew that something must be done. He must be penalized. We all got let out early for Christmas Eve. I skipped the bus and walked back down to where Creature had been. Police and townies were all on the woods. There was no real way i would be able to find him.

I returned home. My mom had been going right on through certainly one of her rounds where she bought food, prepared dinner, and acted out one other time like she didn't just kick me personally. This "happy" cycle only lasts a couple of hours before someone says or does something that tips the scale and she's full-blown again that is crazy. The opportunity was taken by me to eat and go to my room. Not a lot more than an full hour later on after my dad talked about that the gas got switched off did she tip. I started packing a bag for myself. I put on my shoes and left for the door that is front. I needed to get in front of the storm and appear for Creature. The next it was opened by me, my mother's hand slammed it closed.

"Where the hell can you think you're going?" she asked.

"Why would you care?" I snapped straight back.

"You're maybe not going anywhere."

"I'm not planning to sit in this house as you hit and yell at me. I'll just leave."

My daddy walked by us, slinking up the stairs to his room.

"Mom, I'm leaving."

She grabbed me by my throat.

"Tell me personally just what you're planning to do again."

We couldn't breathe. a shoe was taken by her and hit my leg with
it.

"It's your fault we can't pay the bills. All you do is take out into the
street. from us! You're lucky we don't put you"

I felt my lungs tearing inside from the pain sensation. I became a
minute from passing down whenever a crash that is loud the
screen made my mother let go. I didn't need certainly to try to find
my friend after all because there it had been, in my own living
room. It walked in the cup that is broken like Jesus on water. It ran
to my mother and grabbed her and tossed her across the space. My
father arrived downstairs and upon seeing Creature, ran for his
gun. Creature was too fast. It slit my father's ankles in which he fell
down the stairs. Creature put its foot along with my father's belly
until it protruded, disemboweling and squishing him. My mother
tried to run, but Creature tossed a table at her, stopping her.
"Please! Take him! Take him!" she pleaded, pointing at me, tears
rolling down her eyes.

Creature wrung her neck, and with one snap that is final crushed
it. Blood poured from her eyes and nose. I sat in silence taking a
look at what it had done to my moms and dads. The two
individuals who raised me from when I had been a baby. My
parents who loved me, beat me, and told me I was scum, and hated
me for existing. I felt nothing as I looked upon their bloodied faces
for them. I suppose it was at that brief moment that something
else changed. I took Creature's hand so we left my house. We

discovered an Santa's that is old costume I dressed him. A red cap, and a red and suit that is black. He just wanted to belong like me.

Santa had finally come to the town of Asher.

We started within my neighbor's houses. One by one, killing them all. Their screams like a symphony in the evening. We watched as he pulled organs out, smashed people's minds, selected teeth, and splattered blood on Christmas trees.

Oh, how the red brightened the night time that is magical.

I knew I wished to relish the minute whenever he saw who had been behind his death when we reached Dan's house. Creature slashed Dan's father's neck and with its claws that are sharp stabbed his mother. Dan screamed in horror as Creature inched closer to him. I smiled at Dan who looked back with a face i'll forget never. In all honesty, it was a look of defeat. Creature took Dan and limb by limb, tore him apart. Their agony was my cloud of denial and his suffering my liquor and I was drunk in it. We watched Creature feed on some of the systems, offering me chunks of eyeball, brain, and liver as soon as we were done. I wondered where this beast had come from, but it did matter that is n't. He was my friend and he answered my one Christmas wish. A wish only Santa could offer.

Prior to the night had ended, Creature took one last appearance I somehow knew he wasn't coming back at me, but. There was clearly no farewell that is ceremonious this beast went right back in to the darkness from where it came, and I didn't even feel sad. My friend ended up being gone, and I also still felt nothing.

The truth is, we simply wanted to be alone.

When the news headlines hit that a city massacre had happened, the international world was in surprise. The only survivor was a boy that is fourteen-year-old. I told the police no lies that night.

These were told by me that Santa Claus had come to town.

ANOTHER WORKSHOP OF SANTA

Perpetual darkness lingered at the top associated with the world. Thick ice, frigid air, and snowfall covered the mountainscape that is lifeless. Nonetheless, the night time that is endless not go unchallenged. A source that is single of illuminated the sky and drove back the darkness. Nestled between two hill that is snow-covered a little cottage sat with puffy billowing smoke increasing from its chimney. Ignoring the fact that the civilization that is nearest was thousands of miles away, towards the casual eye, the house was merely a warm and welcoming house. Still, one might say to by themselves, "What an odd thing to get in such a spot that is bleak. How could such a plain thing come become?"

Like most things found in the North Pole, not everything is as it seems. The land was cruel and unforgiving. It could take your life within seconds. Only a select number of creatures were given permission to live in this harsh and wilderness that is relentless. All others who entered this domain did it of the own accord; including the residents of this tiny home that is little. However, him or her were like no other and with a little that is little of at their disposal, they lived pleased and joyful everyday lives.

At first glance, it would seem it had been nothing more than a simple, ordinary home inhabited by an elderly couple who enjoyed each other dearly. If this were your conclusion, you would certainly be mistaken. In truth, a secret that is magical below, for the tiny household ended up being much a lot more than meets the eye. The house that is little maybe not just a property but the tip of a mystical workshop hidden under the ice.

For hundreds of years, children round the world discovered joy from the efforts of the workshop that is hidden. All 12 months round, small fingers that are magical and labored to produce toys and playthings for all of the good children for the world. Elves, the final associated with magical creatures from old, dwelt within its walls and utilized their nature that is mystical to wondrous and joyful things for Christmas early morning. Three days following the Winter Solstice, the old guy would put on their heavy coat and boots, take to the air and deliver his Christmas joy to every child that is last.

Like everything in the cosmos, there should be a balance. For every, there must be a day; every start has an end evening. And, with every kind child, there had been a naughty boy that is little girl become discovered.

Far below the lights which can be bright singing, and happy elves producing and building new and fantastic toys, there was another workshop. There, the warmth of the hearthstones could not reach. The other was dark and sterile although the purpose associated with upper workshop was to bring happiness. It too had a purpose. It was right here where the masses of cheap and easily broken toys had been made. There was no love placed into these objects. Never would a eyes which can be child's with wonder and awe upon seeing these gifts on Christmas morning. The old man knew that even a naughty child shouldn't be forgotten during this time period of goodwill in their wisdom. Nevertheless, the man that is old no trick and had no desire to waste his resources on such unsatisfying tasks. This responsibility was handed to the exiled and banished elves that inhabited the deepest bowels below the Workshop. Those with selfish hearts and desires that are greedy. Stripped of their immortality, they wasted away in the dark with only the trinkets and materials that are flimsy pass the time.

Erhgra E'tah sat within the poorly lit corner of a workbench that is tattered. Their focus ended up being entirely dedicated to the old and piece that is worn of in his hands. The clangs of their hammer steel that is hitting out and echoed through the dark halls and passageways. He pounded the brass sheet relentlessly before the metal gradually began to surrender its form and bend to Erhgra's design. Suddenly the hammer flew out from the angry grasp that is elf's. He examined his hand that is limp to will it back into his control. Fury filled his heart as he viewed the flesh that is necrotic off his bony hand. He didn't have time that is much.

Their other side was weak, but nevertheless capable of grasp. He reached into his toolbox and eliminated an extended nail that is warped stabbed it in to the back of their paralyzed hand. He pushed on the nail mind until its tip broke through your skin and emerged through his palm. Immediately, the discomfort shot and surged up his arm. The dense and rigid tendons loosened within his hand, giving him use that is temporary of digits once again.

The elf acquired his hammer and resumed molding the form for the metal plate. With every impact upon the metal, he poured his rage into his creation. Exactly how ironic that the item of his work that is tireless was for the ones he hated the most. Their body that is deteriorating was fast. He possessed magic that is just enough fuel the curse he would cast upon the object. When finished, his gift will be placed with all the other junk toys and trinkets that are cheap. Morning it would make its way to "them" and find a kid on Christmas. The curse will slowly simply take hold and begin tearing apart their lives. It shall channel their essence back into him and reignite his immortality. The object would pass from one child, then to another, century after century.

He had simply left that is enough magic evoke his curse!

Erhgra had when worked and lived above. Like any other elf he loved nothing more than to create breathtaking and wondrous toys and gizmos before him. But, in his heart, he wished that he could keep some of his creations for himself. One time, his eyes fell upon a music that is stunning his friend D'lahela had created. The music box was extraordinary; meant as something special to a King's firstborn. It had been magnificent. Crafted from oak lumber, it bore an gold that is elaborate on all of its sides. When opened, a figurine of three kiddies danced hand in hand to a lullaby that is gorgeous a magnificent Christmas tree.

Erhgra E'tah had never desired anything more in their lifetime. It filled his heart with jealousy. He became resentful that this precious and rare treasure would visit an human infant that is undeserving. The lady that is littlen't deserve it! It should head to him, he thought. So, under address of darkness, Erhgra slipped into the ongoing work area and took the music box.

Not able to rest and anxious to put the finishing touches on their creation that is prized decided to return to the workshop. To his surprise and shock, he caught the elf trying to steal the music box that is special. D'lahela had been enraged, for greed and thievery amongst elves had been exceedingly offensive and not tolerated. Erhgra begged his buddy not to report his transgression, but D'lahela was unmoved by the pleas and looked to tell the other people of Erhgra's crime. Desperate, Erhgra did the thing that is just for him to do. He grabbed a hammer and brought it down on his friend's mind over and over once more until no further life stayed in the human body that is broken.

Despite their meticulous efforts to conceal his criminal activity, he could not escape the sight and wisdom of the man that is old. Humiliated and dishonored, the elf was banished through the Workshop and his precious music box ended up being taken from him and given to the princess that is little. Stripped of his immortality, Erhgra E'tah was cast into the cold and dark corridors of this Other Workshop to pay his remaining days, never to create something that is beautiful. As the times of year passed, his hatred for all young children grew and ate away at his sanity. He gritted his teeth knowing that the young children of guy got everything and he had absolutely nothing!

Hunched over their work, Erhgra feverishly worked to accomplish their masterpiece. He stared down at the anvil and hammered down on the metal. Each strike brought the actual faces of a child into his mind.

"It lives in heat." The dull hammer formed the metal into a cylinder that is hollow.

"It stuffs sweets and treats to its face." Stumpy legs were welded into place.

"It gets every thing it asks from mummy and daddy." A head that is malformed crooked ears took form.

"It gets anything its little heart desires!" The brass surface was scrubbed of grime and debris.

"It gets everything it wants!" Small turquoise stones were affixed towards the brass human body.

"I hate it!" One glimmering ruby that is red was bound to your left part associated with the figurine's head.

"I hate it!" Finally, a second ruby that is red embedded into the surface on the face's other side.

"I hate them!"

In the glow associated with the fire, Erhgra organized the brass figurine. It was a representation that is disturbing of rabbit. Its body was a lattice of crisscrossed brass strips bejeweled with a pale turquoise that is blue at each intersection. Its head was malformed and provided the impression of a thing that is dead of a pleasant bunny high in life. He placed the one thing that is atrocious an open silver locket that contained a mirror on every one of the hinged internal sides. Aided by the rabbit figurine facing one of many mirrors, he carefully opened a vial that held a fluid that is clear. It was lymph. The lymph from an elf was the source of magic that flowed through their bodies like that of blood from the second set of unique arteries discovered within its circulatory system and pumped by a really special heart that is second.

Only some drops which can be small from the vial. It splashed onto the figurine and mirrored locket illuminating them with a glow that is golden. Erhgra closed his eyes and spoke the expressed words of wormwood in his elven tongue. The fluid that is clear black and stained the surface of both the rabbit statuette and silver locket. The radiance switched a purple that is deep slowly faded. Happy with the end result, he gently placed a cloth over the object without making attention contact to obscure it from sight and very very carefully placed it in a box that is little with holiday cheer.

Finished with his work, Erhgra looked to keep, pushing after dark corpses of several elves hanging upside down from the support beams of the Other Workshop. Their lifeless bodies drained completely of every drop that is final of lymph from slit throats. Erhgra's calculation was indeed correct. He'd just enough secret to fuel the curse placed on the item. The elf that is mad and begun to laugh. For the time that is first a very long time, Erhgra E'tah's heart filled with anticipation at the approach of Christmas morning.

The girl that is little in a large pile of torn wrapping paper from the numerous gifts she discovered beneath the Christmas tree. Regarding the of December twenty-second, Gabby awoke previous than everybody else else morning. She went downstairs and glared during the presents that are many continuously tempted her. It was as her every time she looked over the colorful and beautiful wrapping paper when they teased and mocked. She would receive such a scolding that is terrible her parents, but she couldn't wait any longer. At first, it would just be one gift she opened. Then it became two, then another and another. It, all of her presents had been opened before she knew. Despite getting everything she asked for, the desire to have more still ended up being not pleased.

Whenever Gabby stood, a gift that is small to the base regarding the Christmas tree caught her eye. She might have sworn it had perhaps not been there before. The paper that is wrapping worn and yellowed with age. Written in big words had been a tag having said that: "To Gabriella." It was like no other, and she surely would have experienced it before. Puzzled, she eliminated the wrapping paper and discovered a box that contained a smaller package that is sealed a scroll. The scroll ended up being opened by her and read:

Congratulations, happy one! You are the owner that is happy with, the Rabbit. Pepe really loves you and may be your friend that is best within the entire world. Pepe is a close friend like no other, and he can give you everything your heart desires.

To be Pepe's friend, you must pay attention to him, and not disobey the instructions that are following

1. Place Pepe on his locket facing the mirror.

2. Never look Pepe into the eyes. He is ever so bashful and only likes to see you through his mirror.

3. you might ask anything of Pepe 3 x. In three days' time, he shall grant any and all you asked of him.

4. Never look Pepe in the eyes. It bears repeating! He does not like it and certainly will be "upset" if you disobey this rule.

Remember, happy boy that is small girl; Pepe loves you. He really loves you more than someone else in depends upon that is wide. Pepe will be sure that no one will ever hurt you once again. And you may pay attention to him and do whatever he asks of you in the event that you love Pepe.

Pepe loves you, and nobody will come between you ever and him.

Pepe loves you.

AMONG THE STARS: A BOX OF LIGHT

It all started once I ended up being a girl that is little. Christmas Eve, 2004. I had been eight years old.

"Santa, are you?"

Footfalls in the staircase echoed through the homely household as I jumped out of bed and went after the dark doorframe to catch a glimpse of the guy himself.

CREAK

CREAK

CREAK

I waited patiently in the hall just outside my room. An outline showed up at the top of the stairs then slowly made its way to me. The floorboards struggled to hold their weight as the noise of bending wood ricocheted from the walls and burrowed into my ears.

CREAK

CREAK

CREAK

When the figure reached me, its kind ended up being illuminated; bathed within the moonlight that is dim shone through my bedroom window and leaked out into the hallway. My excitement was immediately replaced with pure terror. The thing standing in front of me wasn't Santa, not by an attempt that is long. It was a shadow that is walking a dense patchwork of pitch blackness in the shape of a man. I could neither inhale evenly in its presence, nor could We bring myself to operate, petrified in a continuing state of shock.

Then, he made his move.

Darkness spilled out from the shadow man's hands as he stretched his arms out over me. Soon, I became encased in it; all fading that is light view. Aside from the pounding in my chest, all noise had ceased too.

"Daddy!"

All I could think to complete was call out to my father. Certainly he'd rescue me using this nightmare.

"Daddy! Help! I'm in here!"

Of course, he never showed. Me personally, I became now unreachable wherever we was, whatever energy had enveloped. My connection to the entire world that is outside lost, and I also was alone.

Prior to the inclination to cry or scream further could activate, my tomb broke aside and dissipated entirely, revealing environments that are brand new.

I happened to be home that is n't.

Not close.

***

Despite the circumstances, it was breathtaking. Less a place than it was an expanse that is endless. There were constellations all around; at my sides, above, and also below me personally. The only real thing that separated us was a thin, very nearly clear radiance. It made up a floor beneath my feet, a ceiling overhead, and walls, barely visible in the distance. It was an light that is inexplicable off in certain portion of the universe, partitioned from the rest. An absurd, but architecture that is brilliant in the framework of room.

In admiring the movie stars and galaxies, I took in a sight that is dreadful. The shadow guy was here with me personally, just a yards that are few my position. He bolted within my way and I also ran; faster than I had ever run before. Escape, however, was not an option. We were in a breeding ground that is enclosed. Large that we knew of as it can have been, there were no exits, or at least none. Still, guided by a fear that is pervasive we ran. I ran until my lungs caught fire and my legs offered out.

I collapsed, and that's when he struck.

The predator leaned over their prey that is wounded and his hands over my chest. After that, I happened to be drained. Perhaps not of my energy, but something else. A swirl of glowing particles arose from my own body whilst the silhouette craned his throat back in satisfaction, like a wolf howling at the moon. Their dark, featureless face will forever be etched into my memory.

And then, from me personally, my consciousness wavered as I was nearly sucked dry of whatever it was the shadow sought. In just a few seconds, my eyelids drooped additionally the lights went out. At the full time, I thought it had been death hold that is taking. Also at eight years old, we welcomed it. Anything to end the torment. But, as luck would contain it, this was not death chasing and torturing me in a box that is light the movie stars.

It was one thing far worse.

***

I awoke in bed, my father stationed within my side, trying his best to soothe me.

"Come on, Sweetie. It's okay. It had been just a nightmare."

I wrapped my arms as i possibly could, elated to see him again, when just moments before, I was convinced I never ever would around him and squeezed as tightly.

"It was a monster! It absolutely was gonna get me!"

He pulled my hands away and held my hands in his, looking me right in the eye.

"It was simply a dream that is bad. I won't let anyone harm you, okay, Chelsea? Not ever."

His words were comforting, but he was wrong.

"It wasn't a fantasy. You have to think me, Daddy!"

He smiled and sighed.

"Well, there's nothing we are able to do about it now. I'll leave the hinged door open a crack and you try getting some sleep, okay?"

We nodded and he left, but I did sleep that is n't the rest of the night time. It wasn't a dream. I was certain of that. Every bone tissue in my own body rattled while the skin around them crawled during the thought that is mere of shadow guy and his light box.

It was real. It had been understood by me was.

***

The years went and came. Every Christmas Eve was the exact same. Creaks on the stairs followed by the shadow man taking me to his light box and bleeding me of my entire life force. Then, I would wake in my father's arms me to the very best of his ability as he consoled. No matter how much I insisted it absolutely was all true, my psychiatrist and daddy both believed it to be a nightmare that is recurring absolutely nothing more. Sooner or later, I stopped screaming in the centre of the and pretended to be normal, if for no other explanation than to be treated as a result night.

I told and lied them it was over. From that point forward, no one could ever have to understand but me. It was my mine and cross alone to bear.

More time passed and we grew up. I graduated from college and bought a homely house of my own. The light package stayed we never backed down, outright refusing to allow it get a handle on my life with me every step of the method, but. This attitude gave me personally power in the real face of traumatization, and for a time, it felt like I was winning. 12 months the Christmas Eves didn't get any easier, but worries and misery we experienced in the aftermath that followed was fading faster with each passing.

If this ended up being something I had to call home with, at least I could do it on my terms which are own. It's what she would have desired.

But then, the unthinkable occurred.

***

Christmas Eve, 2019. This could be the holiday that is very first spent in my new house.

CREAK

CREAK

CREAK

The sound was identical to the one from my youth. From hoping each year it would finally be over, particularly now being in a new location for the very first time though I had grown used to the routine, it didn't stop me. Location, of course, did matter that is n't. I ended up being its focus, maybe not the area.

CREAK

CREAK

CREAK

I hid under my blankets since the goosebumps began forming. Being accustomed the routine also did afford me a n't thicker skin in the moments leading up to each occasion. Just I was transformed into an eight 12 months old girl again, frightened for the boogeyman as it started.

CREAK

CREAK

CREAK

It was it. We steeled myself and braced for the worst. The milky, black colored fog then seeped under the covers and engulfed me totally, placing me in an all coffin that is too familiar. From there, the darkness relented and transferred me to that light that is godforsaken in the sky.

Every thing seemed the exact same, just like it constantly had, conserve for starters difference that is glaring.

The shadow man was gone; in his place, a gentleman in turn-of-the-century attire, sitting at a desk.

"Hello, Chelsea. Please, have a seat. It is thought by me's time we talked."

I was floored. This had never ever happened before. There was never any dissonance in past events across many years of being abducted. It was constantly the exact same.

"I'm able to see that you're confused. Please, have a seat, and all will be explained."

The feelings that washed over me personally in this brief moment were many. Relief over not being chased once more; hopeful that it was the end of my many tortured breaks; and even proud it myself, having stood my ground within the years that I'd somehow ended. The one which bubbled to the top most importantly the remainder, however, was interest. That's why used to do as sat and instructed at the desk across from the secret man, anticipating the answers he could offer me.

"Okay, Chelsea. Fire away. What exactly is it you need to know first?"

I pondered a short minute and then asked.

"What is this place?"

The man smiled.

"It's the place where your sort come to rest after expiration."

"Expiration," I asked, "You suggest death?"

"Yes. Not here, specifically, needless to say. This will be just where we harvest energy."

We looked around at the emptiness that is vast.

"Really? There's nothing right here."

The man chuckled.

"Of course there is! You just can't see it. We're a loose assortment of molecules work that is doing a subatomic degree, myself included. I only took this type to make things easier for you personally. Here, have actually a visual representation!"

The man snapped their hands, and all at once the container that is light. We were still at the desk, but were now at the center of a office-space that is massive surrounded by what must are thousands of cubicles, all making use of their own employees, rifling through documents and filing cabinets and answering phone telephone calls.

I looked back into the man, still confused.

"I don't comprehend. Is this heaven? Are you angels? What's happening?"

He scoffed.

"Angels? Heaven? That's just exactly what you humans contact us. Here, we're just celestial overseers on earth that is next. No labels. Just dedication and work."

Nothing was sense that is making.

"Why am I here? Why is any with this taking place in my experience?"

A look was provided by the man of vague concern.

"Well, Chelsea, heaven does not alone run on might. It needs energy to help keep going, plus it is taken by us from people like you."

A man that is brief glasses hobbled over with a stack of paperwork.

"Overseer, what must I do with-"

"NOT NOW, LUCIEN, CAN'T YOU SEE I'M BUSY?!"

Lucien's eyes widened with regret.

"Sorry, Sir!"

He took down into the maze of cubicles, a trail of papers kept on the floor in his wake.

"I'm sorry about that, it's so hard to find help that is great days. Where had been we? Oh yes, energy."

He leaned back in their chair and crossed his hands.

"Despair is the best energy reserve in the universe. One soul's worth is enough to power heaven for years. Because of that, we send operatives out every now and once more to collect soul pieces from humans. You had been the candidate that is next our list."

"Me? Why?" I asked.

He leaned ahead and his lips contorted into a smile that is wicked.

"Your mother's death? Ring any bells? It was a storm that is perfect actually. Your mother moving on Christmas Eve, the when a child is supposed to be at their happiest evening. From that true point on, the holiday was tainted for you. You hurt with every breath you've breathed since, however the anniversary of her death bridges you to our world. It is as soon as your despair are at its top – ripe for collection."

A knot created in the pit of my stomach. As hard it was nothing compared to the pain we felt every single day throughout the loss of my mother, even as a grown-up as it had been to overcome the shadow man's visits. I wrote a letter to Santa, asking for a cure when I was six yrs . old. It is my Christmas gift to higher see her and walking on again. She was taken by the cancer anyhow, and it destroyed us.

Whenever the shadow man first came up those stairs years back, I desperately hoped it absolutely was Santa, him to bring her back so i really could ask.

The rips arrived without warning and damp my face quickly.

"Chelsea! Don't fret! You're one of the ones that are lucky. Most people have actually their soul ripped apart you've lasted far longer than the remainder; well into adulthood until they die and are banished to the ether with all the other abominations, but. Your heart is tarnished, but you nevertheless cling to life with a grip that is vicious the likes of which I've never seen!"

We wiped away my tears and looked back during the man, a expression that is smug across his face.

"So, what is this? You're letting me personally go?"

His laughter that is boisterous bounced the cubicles and rang within my ears.

"Quite the contrary, Chelsea! Given that your soul is damaged, I want to re-map it; insert my pieces which are own build a better weapon. For centuries to come. with you, we are able to extract more energy – enough to maintain us"

My heart sank whenever I realized what he had been saying. The shadow guy. I would become a creature like him.

"No! we refuse!"

"Oh Chelsea, you don't have a choice in the matter."

He snapped his fingers and now we were in another space. I happened to be strapped straight down in a chair and could maybe not move, much as I tried. The person arrived around wearing a lab coat and brought with him a cart filled with sharp utensils.

"Don't worry, Chelsea. This is only going to harm an entire great deal."

We screamed, nonetheless it didn't faze him. He picked up a silver scalpel and carved deep into my chest. The discomfort was intolerable and I vocalized it.

"No need to cry, Chelsea. You have actually an entire lot of tissue around your soul, but I'll get to it, just you wait. It'll all be over soon."

He reached their arm all the way in which into me personally though it shouldn't have been feasible. The pain sensation had yet to subside, nevertheless the foreground was taken by this sensation. It absolutely was truly the thing that is strangest I've ever felt.

"Ah! There it is! Lucien! Bring the pieces!"

Lucien stumbled in with a tray of jars, each with a orb that is faint of inside, and then placed it on the cart.

"Thank you, Lucien. You might leave."

The person awkwardly reached for a jar, his other arm still in my chest. Lucien was still there, watching.

"Here, Sir, let me assist you to!"

Lucien attempted to push the tray closer. It collided with all the man's supply and fell to the floor, breaking every final jar and freeing the soul fragments within, creating an extraordinary disc of light in the exact middle of the room that expanded larger with each moment that is passing.

The man pulled his arm away from my chest.

"God damn it, Lucien! You were told by me personally to keep! If the light from all of these souls reacts she could reconstitute and wake with hers! We'll have actually to wait for the bridge that is next! You IDIOT!"

The light washed within the available room and filled my field of view. I was entombed once again, although not in darkness. It was a energy that is soothing did actually heal my wounds and render me painless. Then, like the darkness it dissipated and transported me personally far, far away before it.

In a change that is strange of, I had been saved.

***

I awoke in the comfort of my bed at house, jumping upright with a gasp that is loud taking in as much air as I could. After gathering some composure, we noticed a burning that is slight my breasts, so

I ran to the restroom, eliminated my bra, and encountered the mirror.

That's when it had been seen by me.

It absolutely was a souvenir from heaven. A scar, right where i'm cut by the man open; a reminder of things to come.

This Christmas Eve, when my despair bridges the space between our globes, I will probably be waiting. However foolish it may be, whenever I'm in heaven once again, I shall stop at nothing to see my mom. Now it is the only thing on my mind that i am aware an afterlife exists.

Mom, over me personally, just understand that I'm coming and I won't allow them to have me if you're on the market listening somewhere, watching. We'll be together again, you, me, and Dad. I promise.

I'm going to bring you back. Whatever it takes.

THE SNOWFLAKE'S DESCENT

Part I: The Snow Fort

Christmas was constantly a time that is whimsical young Christopher. For so long as he could keep in mind, Santa Claus came down the chimney, left gifts, ate cookies, drank coco, and fed his reindeer. Then, he was gone without a trace left out, with the exception of maybe some crumbs and some prints that are hoof. The full time of was mystical to Christopher, and he loved it so year.

Simply like most other child, Christopher had been also obsessive when it came to Santa that is getting in act. Oh, exactly how he'd boast to his buddies when he finally captured a photo of Santa climbing out of their fireplace, or movie of flying reindeer. He yearned for the opportunity, and also this, their desire was particularly single year.

You see, Christopher had an plan that is ingenious. There was clearly no potential for it failing. His attempts in earlier years (four to be exact) had taught him what just will never do. There is no trying to remain awake, listening for sleigh bells, or installing a camera that is video front of the fireplace. No, Mr. Claus was just too clever for that.

This, Christopher would hide outside, in the snow year. After his parents went along to sleep, he would take their father's thermos, with their own coco that is hot and hide in the snow-fort he and their brother built-in the yard. That might be the thing that is final expected! As for remaining awake, he was sure it could be performed by him. All things considered, he was nine now, and he knew just how difficult it ended up being to sleep on Christmas Eve, anyway. But, he didn't want to take any chances. So, he would simply take some fishing line through the storage and tie it to the fireplace home handle, unwind it all then the way in which to your snow-fort. Like that, on him when Santa opened the fireplace door if he somehow fell asleep, the string would tug. Whenever Santa finally appeared, he would get every thing recorded on his older brother's cell phone. Voila!

With bedtime on Christmas Eve, Christopher went to their room to sleep that is feign his parents had attended bed. He lay there for what seemed time without end, until finally he heard the master bedroom door creak shut at the final end of the hall. He lay there another half hour or therefore, ensuring all was quiet, and then crept out of under their quilts. He dressed, took the thermos and fishing line that he had pilfered before, and slunk down the stairs, careful to prevent the dreaded creak in the step that is 3rd the most effective.

The doorway that is front the ultimate test, getting hired open and closed behind him without making too a lot of a racket. Just starting to sweat a bit in his coveralls, he held his breathing behind him, and no lights had come on upstairs until he had closed the entranceway. He walked backward towards the fort, unwinding the fishing line, after which finally breathed deeply when he sat down inside. At last!

Christopher sat looking forward to about an full hour before he felt the sleepiness creeping in. It had been fought by him, but he ultimately lost. He leaned over and went to sleep in the snow, according to his fishing line to wake him.

Couple of hours later, around two into the, Christopher felt a tug early morning. At first, his brain translated it to some sensation that is fuzzy in dreamland, but sooner or later his subconscious jolted him with real world. He bolted upright, fumbling for the mobile phone, heart pounding. He slowly poked his head around the hinged door of the snowfall fort.

Two people, dressed in black, stood at christopher's door that is front.

He froze, unable to think, but somehow knowing that these two were up to no good. Fright overwhelmed him, he wet himself, and he fainted, face-down in the snow.

He awoke a moments which can be few to your sound of his mother's screams.

Part II: Fractals

Chris (not Christopher since his murder that is parent's not spoken to his brother, Jonathan, in almost a year. 2 full decades had passed away since that Christmas, and regardless of how Chris that is hard tried the two just could not get along for lots of days at the same time.

Jonathan had awoken into the middle of the that Christmas to get a snack downstairs, and on his means down the hall pointed out that Chris was out of bed night. He made his way downstairs, expecting to see his brother on the couch, endeavoring to catch St. Nick as he always had. That has been whenever the front door creaked open, and two dark clad men sidled through the door that is front. He ran as fast it missing as he could backup the stairs to their cellular phone to call 911, only to find.

Obviously, Jonathan blamed Chris for every thing after that. The two men had come upstairs while Jonathan hid under some clothes in his cabinet hamper. He heard his mother's screams and ended up being too frightened to turn out. The men had been heard by him leave (with precious jewelry, etc.), and went along to always check their parents…he could not, would not re-visualize that scene. He staggered downstairs and found Chris, within the kitchen, a look that is blank his face and smelling like urine. Jonathan snatched the telephone from him and dialed 911.

Years of therapy and houses that are foster, Jonathan had not found it in his heart to forgive Chris. It was his fault that Jonathan could perhaps not call for help. Their fault that the home that is front unlocked. Jonathan couldn't be in Chris' presence very long without reminding him.

Recently, Chris and Jonathan had decided to meet for lunch. Jonathan was wary associated with the meeting but his wife, Molly, insisted that an obligation had been had by him- Chris was family members. Generally there they sat, in a spoon that is greasy eating fried food that could surely reduce their life in some capability. Into the way that awkward talk that is tiny, the brothers found themselves talking about holidays.

"The wife and I need to get away this, as a matter of known fact, but we can't find an infant sitter weekend. We can get another right time." Jonathan said.

"I could watch the children for the, I'm home week-end. Haven't seen them in a while anyway." Chris offered, over-eagerly trying to purchase some kind of approval, as constantly.

Jonathan didn't stop to think about what he said next.

"I wouldn't be comfortable with that." He stated, abruptly.

Chris seemed Jonathan within the face, anguish filling glassy hurt to his eyes. He wiped his mouth, stood, left twenty dollars on the table, and exited the diner.

That was how they had kept it…Jonathan making a snippy remark and Chris solemnly walking out of an lunch meeting that is currently shaky. Chris had looked at him like a puppy at a newspaper that is rolled. Jonathan hadn't been able to face him once more since.

Meanwhile, Chris tried to proceed with his remedial life.

Oh how he'd hated watching their mother and daddy being lowered into the ground that is cool a grey, snowy time in January. Their bro would perhaps not look him in the eye. The lady from CPS that smelled hair that is like and cigarettes wouldn't even hold his hand. Just what ended up being going to take place to him? Would he and their brother be separated? How come Santa had never appeared- he was partially at fault to be late.

He had fallen asleep in the snow and woken up without parents.

Now back through the embarrassing meal, he pondered the last twenty years of their life as he sat in their cubical at their dead end job for kids-without-parents-that-grew-up-to-be-adults-without-parents. He punched numbers and symbols into a spreadsheet that is monotonous Sentinel Home Security as he spiraled down into his regret and resentment, traipsing a snowflake of repeating fault, despair, and longing.

Christopher was robbed of experiencing joy at Christmastime ever again. His sibling hated him, and for exactly what? Because a man that is jolly fat disappointed him 12 months after year. He could never be trusted. In order to make matters worse, everyone thought it was his fault. They had even tried to tell him Santa was a fake, that he did not occur. They insisted, but that just could perhaps not be true. The chance to live if it had been, Christopher had deprived his parents. No, Santa was no saint. Simply a man that perpetually lets people down.

After the murders, Santa stopped visiting Christopher. Home after home, never again did he receive any such thing he wear their list. Fundamentally, he quit making them. He added Santa to a different list- a listing of people who had abandoned him. He despised the parallel that is phonetic his name and Kris Kringle.

Eventually, Chris figured away that mentioning disdain for Santa earned him quizzical looks from…well…everyone. He learned that thought that is many of Santa as a myth for children, incapable of causing any harm. But just how they had been the death was brought on by wrong- Santa Claus of their parents. He had been an arcane, evil man.

After day, Chris sat in their ringlet of fault and desperation for individuals to understand day. More than anything, he wanted Jonathan to grasp, to forgive him for a crime he previously never really committed.

He passed what might have been the final screen shop on earth as he trudged home one November night in the curbside slush. In it, a television that is 4K How the Grinch Stole Christmas, in most of its Suessian majesty. The theory practically slapped him in the real face, with all of the grandiosity that the period could muster.

Component III: Making Christmas

So easy it was, the thought of imitating Santa Claus, yet so brilliant. Chris might have no nagging problem emulating the man. No, not emulating, but embellishing. A suit was easy to come across, also it is rather inexpensive if he started out small. Money wasn't even really an issue, since Chris hadn't spent expect that is much necessities. Grandiose, but, oh, the joy he would bring! Children and adults everywhere will be convinced of exactly what Chris currently knew.

What's more, he could start with Jonathan's young ones! This would inevitably kill two birds with one stone, as long as Chris could keep their own secret! He would simply sneak in on Christmas Eve, keep gifts, and Jonathan could be forced into believing that Santa had left them. This would prove Chris's declare that their parent's death had been brought on by Santa, because he was real. It had been infallible! All that was kept would be to find a suit and decide what Michael and Samantha wanted. A little would be needed by the latter of reconnaissance.

So, for two months Chris used his luncheon break to drive their Impala that is dying-but-not-yet-dead past household. Each and every time, he would always check their surroundings for onlookers, and then quickly open the mailbox to find it for Samantha and Michaels' letters to Santa. Each time, he would be disappointed. Chris had nearly given up whenever, finally, he started the box to locate a white envelope, addressed in a child's handwriting to the North Pole, with a Claymation Rudolph stamp on the side that is wrong. He quickly pilfered it, and returned to their apartment, filled with pride for his master plan.

The contents for the letter broke Chris's heart, but re-affirmed the need for his mission-

"Dear Santa,

My dad lumber be so mad if he fownd this leter. He says you arnt real and that yore just a real method for grownups never to cept responbulity. But we beleeve in you. I will be only 5 years of age but I no sumthing happened to dad when he was little. Therefore because of this Chrismas we just want something to prove yore real. Anything shall be fine, we just want him to feel beter.

Love,

Michael"

Chris' eyes brimmed with tears, in which he knew that he had to do this plain thing for the youngsters, also as Jonathan. He had doing one thing to assuage this household was being due to the discomfort Santa.

Component IV: There's a Light With This Tree

At last, Christmas Eve had appeared. Chris laid the suit out on his sleep along with the gifts he'd keep Samantha and Michael, an Easy Bake Oven and a Creepy Crawlers kit, both purchased at a vintage doll meeting with cash. Chris thought the vintage nature of the toys were a touch...who that is nice but Santa could acquire may be?! He also knew he required the anonymity of cash...no one could be able to ever show it was him. Yes, he would place the man that is fat shame. A hours that are few now, the children would wake up and exclaim their excitement, while his brother accepted that Chris was expunged of any blame.

Around midnight, Chris put on the suit, and loaded the packages into his car. He drove the ten minutes to Jonathan's neighborhood, and parked a hundred yards across the street, preventing the danger of his vehicle being recognized and seen. He collected the young kids' packages, and walked briskly down the street, careful to avoid the halo of the one street light in his course.

He approached Jonathan's home from the part yard, avoiding the eyes of any night-owl next-door neighbors whom may be up still. He peeked through the relative part window, and found himself gazing into the dining area, through which he could begin to see the living area, devoid of any children staying up to catch the man that Chris now considered a charlatan. Yes, now Chris was the deal that is real. Santa would quickly find himself obsolete.

Then arrived the most important moment of the entire procedure-gaining entry. Once more, Chris had planned well, and in addition benefited from his obvious destiny. Having worked for the safety business, he had offered Jonathan his security system at a price reduction that is steep a previous attempt to get reconciliation. It hadn't worked, but it had provided Chris with the knowledge that to truly save money, the windows that are back not been wired into the system. After assuring that no one remained awake inside your home, Chris slunk around towards the back and began popping off displays and window that is testing. He was beginning to get nervous that he would need certainly to break one, when the second to slid that is last.

"And he blames me for making the door unlocked." Chris mumbled quietly.

The remainder was easy. The window had been closed by him behind him, discovered their method to the living area and began to place the gifts. Then gasp had been heard by him.

Chris wheeled around towards the hallway to the bedrooms and discovered Samantha there, standing with an empty glass (exactly how Suessian!). In complete Santa garb, he waited without breathing to see if he'd be recognized.

"Santa?" Samantha questioned, as she rubbed an eye fixed.

Chris exhaled.

"Why yes, little one," he smoothed, "that would be me."

"i did son't think you were real...wha-"

"It's okay, Samantha! Few do anymore, but I'm happy to have changed the mind!" Chris interrupted.

Chris again waited with no breathing.

"Me too." Samantha said, wide-eyed and evidently desperate for the right things to state to a being that is mythical.

Chris resumed breathing again, the adrenaline fading, so he could complete their plan as he started to consider how to get Samantha back to bed. But just then, maybe the solitary most wardrobe that is regrettable since that one Superbowl took place.

Because the beard that is adhesive from Chris's face, compromised by the fight-or-flight perspiration, Samantha's jaw dropped available.

"Uncle Chris?!" she exclaimed.

"Shhhhhhhhh!" Chris held their finger to his lips her, the adrenaline surging back as he shushed. He thought quickly, desperate to preserve their masterpiece.

Part V: Run Run Rudolph

So Chris resolved to take her. He did not consider the consequence. All Chris could think is that when Samantha informed her father exactly what she saw, his plan would unravel.

"Yeah, Sam, its aren't that is me…why you bed?" he had asked.

"I heard a sound. Daddy tells us that Santa isn't real but I thought maybe he ended up being wrong. Nonetheless it's just you."

The lie came to their lips as a piece that is last of puzzle that locks in with its comrades. Destiny once again, Chris thought.

"Oh but Sam," Chris whispered, "Your Dad says all that stuff in order that no body suspects…I am Santa Claus!"

Samantha's face showed the delight that only an eight old could year. Chris didn't have to try very hard.

You to see the reindeer, right now."If you can keep a secret…I'll take" He cooed.

Samantha nodded with the enthusiasm of a hummingbird sipping Coca-Cola. Therefore Chris took her by the tactile hand, and led her outside, back through the window he'd entered through. He had to keep the plan together, for Michael, and for Jonathan. He took the gift for Samantha as he calculated using them, convinced that perhaps an Easy Bake Oven is a good distraction on her.

He led her down the stroll to the motor car, again careful to prevent the street lamp. Samantha, of course, kept asking why there weren't any reindeer and why he hadn't used the chimney. Chris absentmindedly kept saying he didn't constantly use either as he tried to bring some sort of plan B into focus. The easily procured contentment of an eight old yet again saved him 12 months. He got Samantha in to the vehicle and began to carefully navigate the roads that are freshly plowed to his apartment.

Once there, he told Samantha that him, plans for the night had changed because she had seen. He'd have his elves wind up that she be patient, because they'dn't be able to get back for a day or two to recover them and take them back again to the North Pole for him this year, also it was crucial. He gave her the Easy Bake Oven, and left her in his living that is tiny room he went into the toilet. His plan was just starting to coalesce.

Chris grabbed several of the Xanax tablets he had leftover behind his mirror from his years of psychiatry visits and used a glass to smash them into powder on the counter top. He scooped the powder in to the product that is now empty, and pocketed it. No way would Samantha cooperate when he began driving her out of town.

Next, he went towards the cabinet and opened his Wal-Mart that is little bought. He kept a large amount of cash, wary for the next time the economy crashed as well as the banking institutions screwed everyone...he was in security in the end in it. He'd withdraw what was in his accounts later; the banks would be closed on Christmas anyway.

He went to the tap and filled a glass with water. He poured in the powdered Xanax and stirred into the main space as he took it. Samantha was still trying to puzzle out utilizing the oven, not realizing that the brownie mixes that came along with it were long expired. Water was offered by him.

"Just knew I interrupted you just before got your water earlier."
Chris said, with the voice that is sweetest he could muster.

"Oh thanks!" Samantha said.

She paused occasionally to ask concerns concerning the North
Pole as she drank. Exactly how elves that are numerous there? Just
how do reindeer fly? Just how long does it take to make the gifts?
Chris had a answer that is smooth each, pandering to her as she
completed the cocktail. Finally, the glass empty, it ended up being
taken by him and returned towards the kitchen. He busied himself
with mapping and packing his route to Canada while he waited for
the drugs to take effect. About 30 mins later, he peeked around the
part through the kitchen to the living space, and smiled as he
discovered Samantha sleeping soundly on the flooring.

He hoisted her over his shoulder (just like Santa and his sack!) and
took her to the automobile. He returned once again for the suitcase
he had filled with every one of the necessities. Taking an
additional appearance around to the apartment he knew he would
not see once again, he found convenience in knowing he was doing
the thing that is right.

The car pointed north, Chris had a long drive to the border that is
canadian. He would have to cross three states to get there, but he
had a need to get in terms of he could before anyone realized

Samantha was missing. Jonathan and also the rest of his family would oftimes be waking within the couple that is next of and stay terribly upset, to express the least.

But wait! Oh, how could he have been so stupid?! just what would Jonathan think if Chris had disappeared at that time that is same child had? No, that simply will never do. He would certainly be suspected then, whether or not Michael's gift did its task. No, he had to have a talk with Samantha, get her to comprehend.

He brought the motor car back around to the south. His plan required he be there, as if absolutely nothing had happened. But could he really depend on an eight old to keep his key year? Chris thought maybe not. He hated how complex this had all become. And then, another thought found him.

In the past, Chris had experienced a complete lot of short-term memory loss when he took the Xanax. In fact, that's why he'd quit taking it. What if it had the effect that is exact same Samantha? Even if he could easily get her straight back into her own bed while she was knocked away if it didn't, just what? Then, any such thing she did keep in mind had been simply a really fantasy that is vivid. Short of maintaining Samantha hidden somewhere, it was the only way he wanted out he saw that still achieved the end result.

It is close but Chris had to back get Samantha into her bed. He sped back again to Jonathan's neighborhood, arriving just before five o'clock each day. He took Samantha out from the back seat, and moved since quickly as he could back to the window that is right back. He went first, and pulled Samantha in behind him. Jeez, Chris thought, she was actually out. He took her down the hallway as hastily in her bed as he could while still being silent, and put her. He took one look back, the pride of a job well done swelling in his chest as he left.

Part VI: Ghost of Christmas Past

At seven clock that is o Christmas Day, Michael sat bolt upright in their bed, looked outside at the growing light of morning, and hopped across the hallway to his sister's room.

"Sammy, get fully up, it's Christmas!" he exclaimed.

There is no response from Samantha. Michael pulled the blanket back, shaking her. When she didn't budge, even Michael's mind that is young one thing was amiss. He tried for a few more seconds, and noticed just how Samantha that is stiff was like she was frozen. As fear begun to take control, he went because fast as their short, coverall pajama clad legs would take him to his parents' bedroom.

"Daddy! Mommy! Sammy is sick, she wont' get fully up!" he cried, as he shook Jonathan awake.

"Wh....What?" Jonathan yawned, as he came away from a rest that is deep.

Michael continued to fairly share their dismay, Jonathan never ever anything that is actually thinking incorrect until he got his eyeglasses on and saw the look on his son's face. After that, instinct took over, and he leapt out of the bed.

"Molly, wake up, something's wrong." he yelled, as he strode to the door and down the hall to his daughter's room.

He joined Samantha's room, and knew from her color something was gravely awry. He did what any parent would, shaking her. When that did work that is n't he checked for breathing. There was clearly none.

"Molly, call 9-1-1!!!" his voice cracked, as he started upper body that is performing.

Night part VII: and also to All a Good

Chris got a phone call around noon on Christmas Day, being released of the sleep of a night's work that is full. His sister-in-law spoke as he muttered a hello.

"Chris, something awful has happened,she finished, "Michael found Samantha in her bed this morning…she passed away in her sl- sl-sleep." she sobbed, and after a lengthy pause" She broke down her thought as she completed.

Chris sat bolt upright, his hand over his mouth. What had he done?

It only took a brief moment for him to realize his error. The Xanax was in excess. He'd euthanized her. Tears began running down their face.

"Oh my God, Molly…"

Yet, the self-preservation instinct was strong. He'd to lie it might if he wanted their plan to work, and there is still hope. Eventually, Michael would understand that a gift had been had by him from Santa, therefore would Jonathan. He'd been careful, and his only end that is loose been silenced forever, albeit accidentally.

"What happened, Molly?! Is Michael okay??" he asked.

And so it went.

a later, Chris wandered in to the wake for Samantha, maybe not having to fake sadness- he had loved her dearly week. But she had died for the greater good. Yes, this might be painful for some time to every person, but the end result that is meant of design had already started to take hold.

Jonathan had let Michael open their gifts as a distraction. He didn't know what to make of it. Michael, of course, was convinced it originated in Santa. Jonathan was not. Chris overheard him speaking about it with a few family friends in a tone that is hushed. He approached cautiously.

"Jonathan…I…" Chris couldn't finish.

Jonathan stared at him a brief moment, Chris seeing what was coming. He had made a miscalculation that is terrible.

'WAS THIS YOU???" Jonathan bellowed, grabbing Chris by the tie.

"Wha- what?? just what do you mean?" Chris stammered, retreating.

Several attendees hurried in to pull Jonathan from Chris, Jonathan screaming about the gift, and exactly how he knew Chris had somehow been involved.

"EXPLAIN THE GIFT, CHRIS!!!" he kept screaming, falling to his knees.

Chris cowered, and he fled outside. Molly chased him.

"Chris, I'm so sorry...he's just in so pain...we that is much are." She said.

"It's okay, Molly...he's always hated me." Chris replied.

Molly looked over him, heart broken not just for her daughter but for Chris as well. He was watched by her walk to his vehicle, and then went back inside.

Another times that are few by, and Chris went back to their life. His co-workers sent condolences, his desk covered in cards and flowers every when he came in time. Gradually, he thought, things would turn out how he liked. Jonathan would see no other explanation. Santa would be real, and Chris would receive the forgiveness he'd purchased with Samantha's life.

His desk phone rang. It ended up being Molly once again.

"Chris, the police took Jonathan in for questioning this morning. We don't know what to do" She deadpanned, clearly in some kind of shock.

The autopsy on Samantha had been finished. Of course, her blood had been tested, therefore the Xanax had been there in gratuitous amounts. Unbeknownst to Chris, Jonathan also had a prescription for Xanax.

The police decided they didn't have enough to actually arrest anyone in the end. Jonathan and Molly did seem the type n't to intentionally poison their kiddies, and no one could ask Samantha if she'd taken them on her behalf own. Also, there was the question associated with the gift that is unexplained lending credence that there had been an intruder. Jonathan did eventually come off of accusing Chris, telling him that despite their distinctions, he knew Chris loved the young ones and would hurt them on n't function. The police canvased everyone residing on the street, to no avail. Chris was in fact thorough, and lucky.

That, Chris had been invited over for coffee, Jonathan softened by his grief and Molly still pressing for the brothers to have a relationship february. They sat into the living room, Michael on the floor having fun with his Hot Wheels. Sooner or later, inevitably, the conversation turned to Samantha.

"I sleep that is still can't knowing somebody was in this house and no one will do anything about any of it." Jonathan stated, quietly to avoid Michael overhearing.

He heard anyway.

"Someone had been here, daddy," he said, without even looking up from their toys, "Santa did it. Santa hurt Samantha."

Oh just how perfect, Chris thought.

SHE IS AN UNEXPECTED MAGI

"Donde Esta Santa Claus" was blaring on the radio as Gary crossed over state lines into...somewhere. He lost an eye on where he was hours ago. Somewhere... midwesty. He ended up being driving back East for Christmas. Too inexpensive to fly, he thought he'd take the chance to get to see America, the REAL America. Turns out, most of the America that is genuine was of nothing next to a lot of scenic nothing. No cars on the highway except him. It was late. Dashboard display said 2:17 am. Taking his eyes off the stretch that is endless of, he glanced up at the night sky. For the briefest of moments, he swore the moon looked...green. Squinting, he could clearly see it absolutely was not. Simply a big circle that is ol the sky made of cheese, like they always said. It's amazing what you are actually thought by you see after seventeen hours on the road. He smeared his palm that is open down face, looking to get the sleep away from their eyes by force. The husks of 5-hour energy containers littered the passenger seat. He instinctively reached for another choose me personally up but swore he'd sucked dry the final one about eighty miles back as he remembered. He needed to locate somewhere to crash for a hours that are few. He undoubtedly needed to fuel up. Possibly grab some food. The sign he flew by offering everything he needed, plus the vacuum that is biggest in the continental U.S., had been just too good an offer to pass up.

Pulling into town, he coasted over to the gasoline place. The prices were ridiculous, but Gary didn't precisely have a wealth of options. They must've gotten greedy from all the tourism the vacuum brought in. He had passed away the home that is celebrated as he made his way into town, green and red lights shining on its little placard. Couldn't have now been taller than six foot. The wonder that is eighth of world. As he endured outside his Honda into the cold that is bitter Gary saw the neon glow of an indicator guaranteeing donuts, burritos and hotdogs. His stomach rumbled. Between hunger and sleep, it looked like hunger was gonna come out on top. He looked around as he rubbed his hands together for warmth. Amidst the shuttered shops and grey buildings that made the town that is small he could see a diner across the road. Whatever they got had to be better than, he assumed, day old dogs that are hot. The pump stopped with a gulp that is noisy. He placed it back in its cradle that is gas-soaked his card, tossed the receipt and drove the hundred yards over to the diner.

A cop had been seen by him car parked out front. A policeman that is middle-aged to be dozing inside, half-finished Twix bar at hand. "Guess the donuts at the gasoline station weren't up to snuff." Garry thought, as he slammed the car door shut and pushed open the metallic that is sleek to the diner.

The bell above the door jingled brightly, alerting the diner patrons regarding the arrival that is brand new. Five or six others were spread throughout, munching on curly fries and milkshakes which are slurping. Not exactly a spot that is happening. Gary stepped over to the counter and took a seat using one of the round, bright stools that are red. In moments, he was greeted by a man that is stocky a paper chef's hat. It absolutely was green. Weren't they? that is always white was staring at the hat for a couple of seconds ahead of the man spoke.

"What can I getcha, pal?" He tossed Gary a menu and started wiping his hands on their already apron that is filthy.

Gary didn't bother looking at the menu.

"Double bacon cheeseburger, mid rare, curly fries, two waffles and a coke in the largest glass you've got."

The chef nodded in approval. "You started using it, chief. About 15 minutes."

The cook plopped a football sized glass right in front of Gary, completely shielding himself from view after a couple of seconds. It had been large and plastic, the container itself seemed to shimmy and undulate because of the amount that is absurd of and ice cubes floating around inside. Gary shifted the glass slightly therefore the chef might be seen by him and thank him.

"No problem, bud." the chef casually dropped a straw in-front of Gary. Gary cheated the paper sleeve of the straw and dropped it into the glass. It disappeared instantly, vanishing under all those bubbles which can be dark. Leaning over the relative part of the counter, Gary grabbed several more straws. He fished out the straw that is drowned fashioned them into one elephant trunk of a tool, dropped it to the beverage and greedily began to suck it down. He didn't recognize just how thirsty he had been until that ice-cold lifeblood that is fizzy flooding his system. He was so distracted in caffeine fueled ecstasy; he didn't notice the presence behind him.

"You wanna begin to see the Christ youngster?" the voice said.

"Who? What?" Gary sputtered nearly falling off their diner stool.

"The Christ child…wanna see em?" the man was dressed in an army surplus jacket. It was riddled with stains that drew attention far from hair that is greasy hung about his face in stark patches.

Regaining his composure and his seat, Gary responded to the person "Look, buddy, I'm not an idiot. He's born ON Christmas, maybe not before. If you wanna run a scam, at the very least get the known facts right. I don't have any cash if you're hunting for a handout. I've got waffles coming soon. You need some, they're yours. Simply leave me alone."

The guy that is dirty at Gary, no reaction in his eyes. The other patrons of the diner seemed like they were doing their best to disregard the scene that is entire. A glance had been shared by the grill chef with Gary and rolled their eyes. Nevertheless the guy that is dirty, like a statue, staring at Gary, unblinking. It absolutely was impossible for Gary to ignore the dirty presence that is man's. Finally, he swiveled his diner stool slightly in the man's direction that is dirty.

"Alright, I'll bite. What exactly is it? You attempting to unload some Christmas cards prior to the seasons over? A dog had been got by you in a box out there with a halo stapled to its head? What's the angle?"

The dirty guy smiled, "No angle through filthy teeth. You come away, I explain to you the Christ kid and that he's exactly what I say he is, I pay for your dinner. if you don't believe 100%"

Gary considered the prospect of a totally free and dinner that is obvious. It would cap their stay off in nowheresville and provide him a great story for Christmas supper.

"Lead on, champ." Gary considered the cook as he got up off of his stool.

"I'll take a check when I reunite. This gentleman has generously consented to simply take ca…"

"Not yet." The person that is dirty in along with his unblinking stare.

"Okey dokey, then. Let's go."

The dirty man led him out the doorways associated with diner into the crisp, grey wintertime night. They wandered two blocks across the street, passing the shuttered and empty shop windows.

"It's right down here." The man that is dirty in the direction of an alleyway.

Gary stopped and peered down the filthy, empty passage. Shadows dancing within the trash and discarded pizza boxes. He had a inches being few at least fifty pounds on this guy if he attempted to pull anything. A gun could possibly be had by him or a knife, but he didn't think so. Didn't look like the type that is twitchy. But he didn't want to be stupid.

"Go right ahead, bud. This is a follow the leader situation."

The man's that are dirty never left his face, "Sure, man."

Within the illumination that is dim of part streetlight, they navigated the alley. The man that is dirty him to a small field during the far part, almost touching the brick dead-end. He pointed, "In there. Open it up and you'll see."

Gary maneuvered across the box, so he had his back to the wall surface and was facing the man that is dirty. He looked down at the small, slightly damp cardboard that is looking smiled.

"Free dinner and then back on the road."

The flaps were opened by him and looked in. He stared silently. After a full moment or two, he reached in and pulled something away. It was a shape that is small in big money of torn clothes. Pulling back the cloth covering, a child was revealed because of it. A child with the most striking and beautiful eyes that are green ever seen. Like he was plunged into an ocean of calm as he held the child, Gary felt. Every fear, every worry he had ever endured fled like shadows within the sunlight. With tears welling in their eyes, he turned to the man who'd extended an invitation to meet up his savior.

"You know…I… never really believed…it just didn't seem sensible to me. But this…" He looked down at the child that is smiling "This is practical." An look that is energized Gary's face, "Who else can we tell? Everybody has to understand about this! Everybo…" He was take off by the set that is large of that clamped down and tore away his throat. In his pain and panic, he dropped the kid, its mouth that is tiny stained crimson. Faster than he thought possible, arms reached out to get the child. Arms belonging to the man that is dirty. Sliding down the brick wall associated with the street, Gary ripped off his sleeve and stuffed it from the spurting, open injury on their neck, in a desperate attempt to staunch the bleeding.

"That…that's maybe not the Christ child…" he choked down, struggling to stay conscious.

The guy that is dirty the light tufts of hair on the baby's head as he spoke.

"Oh, it's the christ child alright." He motioned towards the opening associated with the alleyway. The diner patrons, the grill chef, even the sleeping cop he'd passed parked in their patrol car. They certainly were all gathered there, crowding out the light. All staring. Along with their brilliant eyes which are green.

"It's just not your christ youngster, it is ours." The guy that is dirty has his dead-eyed smile. "And every christ child needs gifts. Thank you for bringing the very first."

The thing that is last ever seen had been the dirty guy reducing that…thing wrapped in swaddling clothes down to his level. It gurgled as its face that is tiny split to produce way for endless rows of shiny, red-stained teeth.

A CARROTS AND WHISKEY

The alarm was horribly loud in their remaining ear, a persistent high pitched beep forcing him from his dreamless, alcohol-soaked slumber into a wakefulness that is hangover-heavy. Jim groaned, rolling away from the machine that is insistent negligently silencing it with a lucky swipe of their arm. His head felt fuzzy and thick, his tongue dry and his belly on the verge of rebellion.

Jim opened his eyes and peered at the sliver of cold light showing through the curtains as half-recalled memories danced across his brain early morning. A crowd of his friends in the pub. Reindeer jumpers and a elf that is sexy behind the club –

Oh, god. Morning it's Christmas.

Crazy panic stabbed he turned to his side through him and. Sandra was lacking. The space that is empty him was cold; she'd been gone a while. It had been their change night that is final he remembered that clearly; he'd made her the promise as he'd headed out. Wrapping his scarf around his neck he'd stepped towards the hinged door, giving her a smile and saying that, needless to say, he wouldn't forget. How could he? Christmas Eve was the absolute most vitally important evening of the year, a trip that's basic with buddies wouldn't alter that.

But they'd had a few of drinks, then Harry had recommended a couple more. He'd barely understood he'd had so much until he stood up to head home and almost fallen over. They'd sung some tracks on route back, passed each other drunken warnings about not forgetting to put the carrots down and whiskey, and he'd stumbled in fully going to do so. But then their memory was a blank.

Did they truly are placed by me away?

What if he'd forgotten? Sandra was missing...

Ripping the duvet off he clambered away from bed and hurried to check on Owen. The kid was sleeping soundly, which considering it was Christmas ended up being unusual. He must finally be growing up, which at the age of eight was well overdue. A test of his parents' patience in years past he'd bounded out of sleep at the crack of dawn, thrilled with the excitement of presents and determined in order to make every second of the afternoon.

Jim's heart began to relax its pounding that is manic at sight of their son. He hadn't been taken. He sagged against the door-frame for a moment, recovering his composure and attempting to disregard the frustration that is throbbing his skull. Gradually, he shut the hinged home and stepped back to the hall, enjoying the flood of relief which momentarily washed away a few of the shame.

Sandra was in the kitchen, huddled in her fluffy dressing that is white and nursing a cup of coffee. She looked terrible. Pale and haunted, her hair that is dark hung around her arms and her eyes stared unseeing at a spot far away.

"Morning hun," he ventured tentatively, reaching for the kettle, "Merry Christmas."

Her eyes which can be glazed to his, her expression bleak.

"Merry Christmas? That's what you tell me?"

"I'm sorry, honey. I'm therefore, so sorry." He hesitated, torn between wanting to fill the kettle and not attempting to seem insincere. He shuffled his feet.

"You're sorry," she repeated flatly, turning back to her coffee. "You have no idea exactly what I went through. I woke up, you have there been, snoring away in your clothes." She gave him an accusing, mad glare.

"Good thing we decided to test that you'd done exactly what you said you'd do, wasn't it?"

"Yes," he said meekly, looking down at his feet and feeling thoroughly miserable.

"But you hadn't."

"No." What else was there to say?

"Jesus, Jim. How will you be so careless?"

It would be no reason to say he was drunk. No excuse he only got to see once a year that it had been Christmas Eve and he'd been

using the friends. It couldn't help remind her it had to be him
every damn time that she could have just as easily create the
whiskey and carrots, that there was no reason.

No reason she was permitted to shirk the duty year in year out,
just so him never to be out late that she had a reason to share with.
That is, besides her jealousy that he had friends that weren't her.

He settled on just saying he ended up being sorry once more and
turning away to fill the kettle. To their relief, she said nothing
more about it.

"So, how's it look out there? The news is caught by you yet?"

She sighed, a resigned, miserable sigh. "I didn't have to. There's a
news crew outside the Thompsons'. Appears like they forgot."

Jim turned, the kettle forgotten. The Thompsons weren't really
friends of theirs but they had been individuals who are decent
they got together from time to time for a drink, to discuss their
children or the institution, that sort of thing. To believe they had
been gone, taken by the demon for the crime of forgetting to
placate its demands being strange was horrifying.

"Jesus," he breathed.

"Could've been us," Sandra stated. It absolutely was accusatory that is n't just factual. Her face was that of a person who'd just been taken back from the edge of a cliff; ashen and wan, her eyes wide and staring as her narrowly avoided fate playing out before her though she could see.

He crossed the kitchen and hugged her, feeling a sort that is new of when she hugged him back tightly and sobbed into their t-shirt. They endured that genuine method for some time, neither one going, their minds playing out of the horror of exactly what might have been, until Owen arrived bouncing into the kitchen clutching the case of presents he'd bought at the conclusion of his sleep.

"Mummy! Daddy! Father Christmas came!" he enthused in that way only very children which are small, dragging the sack over.

For a second, Jim couldn't summon the parental good cheer he needed, struggling to put the near-miss towards the back of his mind and drag his Daddy-At-Christmas persona up. In a way, him to admit it, he was anticipating to when they no longer had to pretend though it pained. When Owen would be old enough to finally learn the truth concerning the creature that clattered across the household on Christmas Eve, the being that parents around the globe conspired to portray as a present-giver that is jolly order to prevent conversation of dark truths too terrible for young minds. The perfect, universal lie that sent kids running early to bed regarding the one night associated with year inside their rooms feigning sleep if they heard any strange sounds during the night that they were most vulnerable, and kept them. Generally it didn't bother him but this morning, having come therefore close to disaster, it had been harder than usual to put the spin that is essential the beast that had visited them into the night. Specially when he'd spent so hours that are many up all the gift suggestions he now had to attribute to a thing that had very nearly murdered them all.

"Wow! Lucky you, honey!" Sandra finally said with a convincingly excited gasp. "Go ahead and just take your sack to the living room and we'll see what he " Her eyes met Jim's and mouthed the words 'get it together'. Owen, oblivious, ran off happily pulling their sack of presents behind him.

Jim nodded and took a breath that is deep as Sandra followed their son in to the family area.

A minutes that are few he was standing by the window, staring at the audience away from Thompsons', making appropriately encouraging reactions to their son's wild cries of pleasure and exclamations of exactly what he was going to do with his toys. The news crew was solemn, and to their rear the police were taping off the hinged doors and windows of the house. No ambulance had been called. There would be no figures. There never ever were.

The headlines had been playing at a dim amount on the TV him, linking him to the horror outside in flashes of juxtaposition to the joy his son had been experiencing inside behind them, but snatches of the report were getting right through to. He had been produced by the comparison feel sick.

"Once again," the reporter said behind Jim, for the reason that light but strained voice they always used to supply these reports, the tension only noticeable by adults, "this Christmas has offered us the highest number of visitors since records started. Some speculation has centered on our population that is growing for figures, but it appears clear that a large proportion of visitors had been from newly arrived migrant families. Some people just forget to alter their Christmas traditions… whilst it is common knowledge that the visitation requirements do differ from country to country"

"Daddy?" Owen asked chirpily from behind him. Jim turned to see that the TV had been watched by the boy with interest.

"Yes, Owen?"

"Why do some people head to see Father Christmas and others don't?"

Sandra caught his eye, offering an shake that is very nearly imperceptible of head. He seemed away, wondering if this might function as minute to let the child in in the truth that is horrible. Was that the point that is responsible do?

"Well,they get to go and see Father Christmas" he stated, calculating his words, "if people don't put out their carrot and whiskey, then. So it could happen to anyone."

"Why don't we go then? I'd like to check out. Can we go next year?"

Jim looked over Sandra. She looked away.

"But we don't need to go to see Father Christmas, Owen. He comes to us. That's why Mummy put out the whiskey and the carrot last night." He pointed to the plate that is little to the Christmas tree and the shot glass next to it. The cup was empty, and Jim had absolutely no intention of using either the glass or the dish ever again. A stuffed that is goofy-looking had fallen over the plate, no doubt knocked by the talons associated with beast since it reached for the carrot. Jim shuddered to imagine it, delicately lifting the carrot off the ceramic without making a mark.

"When did you do that Mummy?" asked Owen, peering round at his mother over a stack of shredded wrapping paper. "Did you obtain to see Father Christmas?"

Sandra gave a laugh that is sickly looked more like a grimace and shook her mind.

"No, honey, I just came night that is downstairs last place a glass of whiskey next to the carrot your father put out."

Jim's heart almost stopped. He stared at her, wondering if that ended up being meant to be some type or kind of joke. From somewhere far away he could hear their son babbling, but the expressed words no longer made any sense. Sandra ended up being Owen that is viewing indulgently shaking her head at something he'd stated.

"You didn't create a carrot?" he managed to say, just about maintaining his voice from rising into a shriek that is hysterical. She looked up, her face now using a expression that is similar usually the one he imagined was on his.

"What?" she said sharply, her eyes dropping to the little dish and widening in sudden, awful realization. Jim's belly tightened in a knot that is cool.

Owen did actually get on the stress that is unexpected his expression curdling like sour milk. He began to breathe for the reason that way that is heavy together with his shoulders moving, that his parents both knew preceded a tantrum.

Jim seemed down, the pieces suddenly falling into place like a nightmare jigsaw that is horrific. The little stuffed snowman, his long, orange, stuffed nose across the white plate that is ceramic.

His wife that is exhausted mistaking for a carrot… putting out the whiskey and going back once again to bed…

"Oh, dear god," he whispered, as a voice that is thick deep with hatred and dripping with obscene desire, gurgled at them from within the mound of discarded wrapping paper.

"Ho, ho, ho," it cackled.

As the wrappings that are colorful outward, Owen screamed.

A FACE MASK REQUIRED

The stillness wakes me. Not that pleasant quiet after a winter snow, or the silence that is comfortable of resting house, but a heavy blanket of non-sound, as though perhaps the atmosphere ended up being afraid to stir. I lay in bed, hardly breathing, straining to get perhaps the style that is slightest. Absolutely Nothing.

Slowly I rise, perhaps not wanting to break the spell. Why could it be every action seems so much louder when you're trying to be quiet? Even my breathing sounds harsh, my pulse thundering in my ears.

I pad to your screen, foot chilled through the lumber floor that is refined. The morning that is early bathes the landscape in weak, yellow tones. Snow glints and contrasts with all the pine that is dark lining the path from the home to the river. Leaning closer the coldness could be felt by me outside seeping in along the frame. We reach out to touch the glass, but my weight that is shifting makes floorboards creak. We freeze set up, suddenly apprehensive, as i'm awake if I don't want anyone to know.

'Is that you, dear?'

A call from below frees all from that stillness and suddenly sounds rush in; the chittering of birds on the deck, the murmur that is faint of heater, the clink of a spoon in a glass. I let a breath out I hadn't realized We was holding and shake off the past dregs of rest.

'Yes, Mum, be all the way down!', I call as I finish making the bed.

I'm home, or at the very least inside my parents' house, for Christmas. We decided, my partner and I, if I arrived up alone, because the edges were nevertheless closed to foreigners because of the virus so it would be easier. To be honest, it was a nice change of pace, and I had truly missed being in a clime that is snowy christmas.

Through the room associated with door that is half-closed glance into my parents' bedroom and think I see a body-shaped lump nevertheless tucked beneath the blankets. Funny, Dad is usually the very first one up. First-time for everything, i suppose.

I gradually make my way down the stairs, pausing to consider the imaginative art Mum had lovingly hung. A piece that is little each place they'd traveled to, a handmade souvenir to be enjoyed in the place of filled into a drawer never to be seemed at again. One time they'll have the ability to include ones that are brand new.

Pausing during the landing a smile that is little across my face as I glance during the tree while the decorations regarding the mantel. Another treasure trove of nostalgia; we'd collected the decorations over decades. It was always fun to determine the theme and reminisce as we unwrapped each bauble that is little.

I across the corner, surprised to see Mum at the dining room table rather than her perch that is usual in kitchen. 'Good early morning!' We chirp her, but… it doesn't feel right as I hug.

'Good morning, honey.' We pause and my arms slacken.

'Are you ok that is experiencing?' I pull back to see her face. Her eyes meet mine and something cold and flashes that are flat, here and gone so fast I must have imagined it.

'Never better! How come you ask, sweetheart?' She smiles and pats my hand, a gesture both alien and familiar. I step right back, nonplussed.

'Oh, it's nothing. Things just seem a… that is little. Should have had a dream that is weird me from sleep.'

'Well, involve some tea and toast, kiddo; that'll set things aright.'

Grateful to concentrate on the task that is mundane of my break fast, I linger on each step. Still incapable of fully shake the weirdness off, I mentally have the day's activities we have planned. So, we're gonna play some Scrabble, then bake the butter tarts and meringues. We root around in a number of cupboards, finally choosing the honey beside the flour into the pantry.

Then… then head out for an appropriately socially distanced lunch at 'our' teahouse. Yum! Another search turns up the butter on the windowsill by the sink. Hmm, and maybe regarding the method home grab some Chinese from that place that is amazing the village. Yeah, this'll be great!

Satisfied with my work to brighten my mood, I spare a watch out your kitchen screen, across the white expanse outside, the snowfall glittering against the bright sky that is blue. I take a good deep breath that is deep carry my cup and plate to the table, determined to keep in good spirits. Smiling at Mum, I drizzle honey over my nicely toast that is charred gladly tuck into brekkie.

'Oh,' she says gently, 'by the way, Dad stepped out. Said he desired a mask that is new the one he's using now is too old.' I laugh because that's so Dad. Anytime he'd pass right in front of a mirror he'd playfully preen and give himself a thumbs up. Now he had been all about collecting masks that are stylish coordinate with his outfits.

But wait... 'Isn't he still sleeping? I thought he was seen by me in bed.' Mum's smile falters, then again comes back, bigger, brighter.

Did she constantly have such a mouth that is wide?

'Oh, silly me, of course he's nevertheless resting. We meant he'd be going out. Later.' She takes a sip of tea, slurping, offering me a glance that is sidelong. We absent-mindedly take another bite of toast, feeling unsettled, a frisson of electricity flitting across my shoulders and the general back of my neck.

Another slurp, and another appearance. Is there something wrong along with her face? The side that is right just like it's sagging. She reaches across and pats my hand again, her hand clammy, bony. Can it be a stroke? We look more closely, attempting to see the telltale signs.

After which, its noticed by me. a slim, red line just below her jaw by her ear. Wha-? Exactly what is that? 'Mum, what's that on your throat?'

'What would you mean, sweetheart?' A pause. 'Kiddo?' Another pause, then in that tone whenever you've determined the key, 'Dear.'

'Is… is that blood?' It's seen by me more demonstrably now, the line. It is tracing along her jaw, spreading, widening. 'Oh, god, what's wrong with the face?' My voice falters; catches in my throat. It's hard to swallow.

She gracefully touches her hand to her throat, peering wryly at the smudge left on her hands like it is an inconvenience, a frustration that is little.

'Sometimes with older ones they don't stay right, you need to adjust.' A laugh that is soft a sigh, and then she straightens inside her chair. I'm freezing and flushed, cemented to mine.

Still smiling that too-wide grin she grasps one hand to her face and casually pulls, —What?—, her face coming away with a squelch, —WHAT?— ribbons of sticky —just what is TAKING PLACE?— ichor suspended between, rivulets of claret trailing down her neck.

'What the f—', I stammer.

'Language, dear', the thing holding my mother's face says.

With a grunt of work I fling myself straight back through the dining table. Can't breathe, can't bre—, no, no, no, no, no, no, I don't—

'It's alright, dear, you'll view it will all be alright' it says so they once again lie seamless against her —its, ITS— epidermis as it gently puts her face back on, smoothing the edges. I lurch out from the dining room, feet moving like molasses, like in a horror movie, —a film! A dream? This is not genuine!— while my turns that are not-Mum her chair to watch.

I hear a thud from upstairs, knowing now it's not my father but another thing that is. I choke back a cry as I stumble towards the front side door.

'Remember dear, if you prefer to stay safe out there...' a chuckle that is low.

My fingers brush the handle that is cool then I'm gripping it, switching it, feeling the icy atmosphere since the door cracks open. She, no, IT, continues to be during the table, watching, amused by my terror, my flight.

So close, it can be made by me! The entranceway, open wider now, allows the cold temperatures chill wash over me. My foot touches the mat that is welcome. Oh god, I'm free. I'm safe.

a breath, a blink, and a movement therefore swift and fluid it doesn't even register. Then, a whisper, soft and ticklish against my ear, '...face masks are required.'

IT WAS GHASTLY WARNINGS

23, december 1975

Brookfield, Montana

1 AM

To John, it didn't seem as if it was going to get colder. But to their dismay, it did. The temperature regarding the train he rode on reported it was 45 degrees, even with all the heaters. The train with its beautiful Christmas designs was an sight that is extraordinary see. Garland hung along the windows, with a haze of red and lights which can be blue around it. The walls were an orangish-yellowish color, giving the inside a comfy, warm feeling. It gave John flashbacks that are a few his family.

Waking through to Christmas Day, seeing his grandkids and kiddies, eager with excitement to see what Santa brought them this 12 months. Of course, Santa John that will be more with excitement to see his family cheering and laughing with Christmas joy. It warmed John's heart. Even if he had been in his very early 30's, his heart was of a man's that is 60-year-old. His smile was comforting and warm. His family used to produce fun of him, as his eyes use to crease as he smiled. He no longer takes offense to it, and treats it as a grouped family memory. His thought process was interrupted, as the snow was noticed by him dancing contrary to the window. The train had stopped. He waited for the conductor to come and tell which stop they had been at. He wasn't an man that is impatient so John could watch for hours. The conductor with their overcoat that is blue and came into the area, shutting the door behind him. He adjusted his scarf around their neck and uttered the language with a croaky tone that is loud "52 Brookfield, Montana stop is here."

Hearing the address given made his ears prick up. He was one stop away from being in town and seeing his family. He gathered his suitcase and strolled onto the platform. What he noticed instantly about the terminal was him being the soul that is just. Empty, cold, and dark besides some Christmas lights hung over the terminal. The train with its horn blasting in the evening faded into the darkness that is snow-covered. Looking around made John uneasy. The deafening silence made their blood run cool. He then began to pace, waiting for the train that is next come. His persistence was surprisingly beginning to run slim. Every drop that is little of icicle, or the clanking of the lights brushing against one another, was loud enough for dogs 10 kilometers away to hear. Suddenly the radiant red lights above gave off an haze that is intense. "Leave now!" a voice echoed. It sounded as though it was using the wind. And that's what he blamed it on, until it came once again, this right time louder. It absolutely was groaning, very nearly moan voice. John through most of his life believed in the paranormal. Just year that is last the entire Ghosts in Amityville business with that man whom murdered his whole family in cool blood.

"Of course, thinking such thoughts isn't an thing that is ideal do right now," he believed to himself. He began to pace a faster that is little. The wind that is blowing gave ghastly howls began to offer him a chill up his back. He didn't understand his sense of dread. But then again the globe today, would give you this feeling. He tried to blow the feeling off, but yet it continually wrapped itself around him like a blanket. Now their pacing stopped, and he begun to pay attention to the wind. Its whispering howls were nothing short of horrifying. As the wind escalated, the familiar voice that is ghost-like back, this time seeming to speak to him directly. "Don't follow," it howled. "Don't follow!" The voice seemed to have others surrounding it. The one which he could comprehend was crying, "Red roses!" It had the pitch of a girl that is little but was nevertheless hard to pronounce, as it whistled with all the wind.

Their feet suddenly felt the desire to operate. But where you can? He wasn't familiar with this particular right part of the state. The red haze from the lights above him, which grew because bright as the sunlight, now seemed to have died down in intensity, along with the voice that is ghost-like. That's when he heard footsteps just behind him. He turned around, white in the face, terrified he would see a lady that is ghostly. Nonetheless it was instead a wrinkly lady that is old. Close sufficient. She gave a heartwarming look, and stuck her hand out, waiting for an handshake that is unnecessary. It was shaken by him rather uncomfortably. Her hand felt brittle, additionally the skin ended up being super slim. The bones had been penetrating all certain areas of this woman, and the coat she wore covered her entirely. He felt he had been shaking the tactile hand of death himself. Finally, she uttered some expressed words, breaking the silence between them.

"Are you alright, sir?" she asked.

"Yes, I'm fine, miss. I'm just looking forward to the train into town."

The woman looked at him dumbfounded. Looking she shook her mind in disbelief around him.

"Oh, you can't be severe?! Come, come, I have an Inn nearby," she reported eagerly. She then swung her hand out to a trail simply beyond the terminal, which led into a patch of forests just beyond that. The outline for the forest is all he could see from where he stood. He squinted producing the crease marks across the relative part of eyes, in an attempt to see the path. The Christmas lights scarcely provided any illumination to the darkness right in front of them. But John nevertheless shivered at the statement. He ended up being no trick whenever it found premonitions or events that are foreshadowing. The ghastly howls he heard within the wind gusts, were warning him of this occasion that is precise. But, against their better judgment, he started to check out the brittle woman throughout the platform and down onto the path that is snow-covered. It had been freezing, and he hadn't had anything to eat since 7 this morning.

His mind chose to ignore the demand to move, but there he was walking alongside the girl that is elderly the trail, fading into the darkness.

* * * * * *

The woods enclosed the two souls walking along the path. The moon was now their source that is only of. John had been thankful that their walk did need to have n't conversing with each other to break the silence. The wind did that. It kept coming until it did, as the elderly woman tumbled in to the snow and landed right on her straight back at them from all sides, seeming to try and knock them down. John quickly picked her up and asked if she was okay. She replied with a firm "yes" while angrily staring towards the wind, which was picking right on up speed.

Finally, the warm colors of a mansion that is victorian. Its bright Christmas lights danced along the shutters and columns on her front porch. For just a building that is two-story it looked breathtaking from afar. Simply safe enough to walk into and enjoy some company. Simply secure enough. The entranceway leading into the house had a beautiful lit that is red hanging along the window. John feeling eager cuffed his fingers toward the glass and peered in through the doorway. The girl that is old smacked his hands away, as she stuck the main element into the home and opened it.

"Very cozy," John stated as he joined the foyer that is yellow-colored.

"Yes, it is. I got myself the homely house just for this reason alone."

"Do your home is here alone?" He asked.

"Well used to do have a husband who lived here, but h-he-he had... um... passed... a years being few." She replied hesitantly. She started initially to cry. Maybe not obnoxiously, simply soft whimpering that is simple. Now feeling pity for the woman, John did want their foolish n't feelings of cautiousness to overtake his mindset. And so he gave the now weeping woman an hug that is embarrassing. Now feeling good they continued in to the home about himself.

Stepping to the hallway, he came to your area that is first the left. It was a brightly decorated area that is residing. Some mahogany futons lay near their side that is right with a glass stained table. Straight ahead was the Christmas tree, positioned beside the fireplace that is already burning. John sooner or later seemed towards the girl, who endured uncomfortably close to him. They both sat regarding the futons and glared at one another. The silence that is awkward them was a lot of. Finally, the silence was broken by him by asking, "Have you lived here alone since their passing?" She responded with a relative mind nod, still not breaking her gaze. Due to the fact discussion seemed to up be lightening, it was once again taken to a halt as the woman asked, "How long do you want to remain?"

The question just kind of seemed out of spot, as she knew that would've only wished to stay for a time that is quick. Probably 'til the early morning. Again silence that is awkward the room. He attempted to correct it by asking exactly how time that is much took her to put all these decorations up. But before she could answer, the bell of the grandfather clock sitting within the foyer rang out. Finally, he had expected for a bedroom. John was extremely much exhausted from the walk that is five-mile took from the terminal. Growing a tremendously smile that is peculiar she ushered him back into the foyer. She then proceeded to pull a podium and a written guide out of a closet underneath the stairs. For an lady that is elderly she seemed rather strong. Sitting the podium down, she handed him a pen to use.

Writing his name down, the visitors could be observed by him before him. What hit him most was that the guestbook included names that are male. Surely there had to possess been couples or at minimum women staying the here night. It was odd. The woman had been odd. This example that is entire odd. But he was tired, and his sense that is common was longer working. He looked up at her after he finished composing his title down. She was smiling. But it was a smile that is weird. It had such a intent that is sinister it. And it gave John that similar feeling that is sickening. Finally looking away she stepped eagerly around to the staircase and headed upward to the second floor from her. Walking up with her, John finally tried to begin a conversation.

"So, how long perhaps you have been in company?" he asked. She hesitated as her footsteps stopped. He could see her face, it was a look that is concerned. She seemed never to know what to express. John currently felt the flags being red. But this ended up being one that most people would've run from. Seeming to act as if there is nothing wrong, she answered, "Well, quite a while now, though I don't really know the quantity that is precise of." Before questioning any further they made it towards the floor that is top. It had three rooms. The room on the left was a small staircase leading to the loft, the middle space was the designated room for guests, while the other on the right, had been an room that is extra. She gestured her hand out to the middle room, and put his suitcase inside the area that is darkened. She flicked the light on and looked he entered the room at him as. Standing into the available room, it seemed rather cozy. The bed lay on the best with the window simply above it. As well as in the far left was a simple Christmas tree, offering the area a beautiful green and tint that is red. Some hot cocoa?"Do you need anything" She asked rather persistently.

"No, but is there a restroom?"

"Not upstairs, but there is a bucket somewhere in here. Goodnight." She replied quickly. She then shut the door and John heard the sound that is sickening of door being locked. He rushed to the hinged door and began to yell.

"Hey, why did you lock the door!? Hello?!" he screamed. It was the final flag that is red. No further was he staying right here. He started initially to violently shake the door, hoping it would break from the hinges which can be rusted held it to the frame. Pounding, and pounding to your wood. The sound of wood splintering ended up being music to their ears.

That's until the haze regarding the red Christmas lights on the tree expanded in intensity. Brighter and brighter it grew with lighting. Now catching his look, John sat in surprise and somewhat amazement at the sight unfolding right in front of him. That is, before the howling that is familiar of wind came back. But now it absolutely was more of a metallic, echoing screech. Also it came from the haze that is red the tree. The haze proceeded to rip it self off the tree, and morphed into a figure that is fog-like. Finally it grew into the design of a lady that is little a 1940s nightgown on. Along with her locks in a braid, but the ends of the haze that is glowing tentacle-like, very nearly similar to solar flares, except red. The screech that is metallic was arranged into the soft sound of a little girl from earlier that evening. John remembered the Christmas incident that is light the terminal. Now realizing it was a spirit getting his attention. It intrigued him, yet still had been terrifying either way. The spirit's messages now gained composure and spoke plainly now than prior to.

"Hush, and please shush! For she is listening!" the reverberant voice whispered. "Why do you come here?"

John couldn't find the words that are proper say. All that came out was a soft, we should ask you the same." I believe"

"Where I stood, you stood," she answered softly. "Until my body fell into the flowers below."

"Were you killed?" he asked. Their brain instantly had the idea of the woman that is elderly. It would make sense, since she seems to appear once this woman that is strange and goes. He couldn't assist but wonder if he had been to be her next target. Once more the spirit knocked him off his train of thought, with another warning that is possible.

"You must be clever, for she thinks one to be asleep," she whispered. The character then started to fade straight back into the tree, along with the haze that is shining accompanied her. But there were questions being nevertheless numerous John had, for the lost spirit.

Realizing why the spirit had left was instantaneous to him, as he heard from outside the door, the horrifying steps of the woman that is elderly. In which the steps we're going, was a question he did want to find n't out. So frantically, he moved the bed from the screen, creating a noise that is screeching the hardwood in the process. He started to attempt to raise the window up, but it wouldn't budge! He looked to your general sides, and of course, they were nailed shut. He looked for the bucket then, to see if he could bust the window pane. He got in his hands and knees to appear under the bed. He quickly covered his mouth from screaming.

Lying there was a corpse, that of a guy that is old. He could tell by the hairs which are gray his blood-covered head. A suit had been worn by it. Together with physical body was covered in smudges of wet dirt. It had been stinking abundantly, and skin had been rotting. He then remembered the spirit's warning, and it gave him an basic idea arrived to his head.

Swiftly he pulled the real human anatomy out of the sleep. He then picked the physical body up from a floor. It had been so stiff and feeling that is empty. It had been instead simple to throw it in the bed. Now getting the blanket, he began to lay it over the corpse that is lifeless headed underneath the bed; well before he smudged some dust and blood around his face and hands. Just as he slid under, the hinged door opened. The woman's that is old bare feet, tip-toed to the bed. From exactly what he could see, the woman was using a nightgown that is dark along side a white veil that draped her arms and head, covering her face. He swears that he had been looking at death himself. Breathing greatly, he waited for a sound to happen. It was abnormally peaceful. Then without caution, he heard the noise of a cracking skull that is constant. Oh, how it delivered chills down and up their spine. However it was nothing compared to the sound of the cover being lifted off the bed. He knew he was caught. That's when the boney hands of the woman wrapped round the side of the bed.

He knew he ended up being good as dead, until an idea that is brilliant to him, like magic from god. Placing his feet in the underside of this bed, he threw it up into the air, smashing the girl to the wall, and giving out a scream that is hellish her. Their feet galvanized him as he rushed to the window. The woman that is shrilling quickly behind. She covered herself as they smashed through the windowpane, and dropped onto the roof of this porch below around him, taking a bite out of his throat. Glass shattered every where, combined with sounds for the wind howling its moans that are awful. Along with the wind came the familiar haze that is glowing except this time it had been shining from all over the house. Penetrating any windows; it delivered beams of red all through the evening that is darkened. And finally there came the whispering voices of not merely the girl that is little but other voices. They were all masculine, combining into a weirdly chant that is melancholic of. Possibly, these were those of one other residents of the homely house, whom she may have killed, or probably did.

Returning to his dilemma, John achingly rose off the roof, with a few bits of cup embedded into the relative part of his face. The girl, now groaning in pain, went swiftly towards him with an item of cup in her hand, which bled from her grip onto it. Attempting to flee her was unsuccessful, as he slipped on the rooftop that is icy. On him, slamming the glass continuously towards any inches of skin she could see as he slammed right back onto their mind, she pounced. Tearing and slashing is all he could hear, as he attempted desperately to block her death blows as she sliced several lacerations on the interior palms of his hands. Unexpectedly, the small girl's spirit appeared, seeming to have the attention of the girl that is old. But sadly, not for long, at it once more as she was back.

One laceration that is final his cheekbone, gave John the adrenaline to toss the crazed psychopath off of him. She then tumbled off the roof, dragging him along, as they both now fell on the wood railing below. Simultaneously, as the haze that is red, additionally the wind became less rigorous. Then every thing went black colored.

A hours which are few, he awoke. Looking around, his vision ended up being blurry, and his breath was once once more calm. He seemed to have landed in a bush. Thankfully, one without thorns. As soon as his vision became clear, he could make down the impaled body associated with lady that is old blood dripping from her lips and nostrils. But when he noticed where the bloodstream landed, he scoffed. They dropped on some roses which are white beside the porch, turning them into red roses. The small girl's caution that is last. Rising from the ground, he limped toward the increase for the sunlight early morning. With a layer of fog on a lawn, additionally the cool that is sharp dancing on his lacerated face. He walked, toward freedom, such as the dead rising from their graves. Freedom from their torment, an utter nightmare that is horrible wishing to be awoken from.

It was the Christmas season. It had just gotten dark, as I was finally able to leave any office that after working overtime night. The roads were damp from the hefty rain; it had been an winter that is unusually warm. I stopped downtown for some Christmas shopping for the kids, just some shopping that is last-minute every thing closed. It was impractical to find a parking i'm all over this the square, therefore I had to park an excellent three or four blocks away whenever I first arrived. I finished my shopping after one hour, got a toys that are few the kids from a few of the local shops, and I started to walk back to my automobile. My feet squeaked and splashed against the dampened sidewalk with each action that is passing. The atmosphere was chilled that; fortunately, I remembered to put on my trench-coat that night evening. It was still cold as hell, but We pressed onward nonetheless to my vehicle down the wreath covered light poles, blinking colored lights and Santas that is dancing in store windows.

The shopping bags at hand, I quickly arrived upon a alley that is darkened. I didn't think much of it; it was like just about any alley, why bother considering it? Besides, I've seen lots of movies to understand that heading down a darkened street at evening was a idea that is terrible. It wasn't so much the ambiance which frightened me, but what I heard. I tried to ignore it in the beginning, I could still hear them when I got to my car just further across the street away from the alley, after which place the bags away in the backseat, but the sounds coming from the alley had been so loud. It sounded like two men arguing with each other, but I couldn't make out what these people were saying. One sound was clearly more dominant one than the other, as it had been louder and angrier while the other was meeker, dropping practically silent against the noises of Christmas music blasting from the radios and also the roars of car engines far in the distance. I couldn't explain it, all I can say was that curiosity got the better of me, and I walked up back the road and down the alleyway.

I pulled my iPhone from away from my coat pocket to use as a flashlight since the lights in the alley didn't work for some reason that is weird. They certainly were here, all intact and in a row, but none regarding the lights were on. Then I was then taken by complete surprise once the phone lit up a face that is gruesome. I immediately slapped my free hand over my mouth to silence the gasp that is unexpected however, once I calmed down, I understood it wasn't real. It had been just graffiti, plastered onto the damped, red brick wall to my left was a face. We sighed in relief after realizing exactly what it had been, but even that didn't relieve me. Artistically, it ended up being good, great, but it was so damn grotesque. The picture ended up being of a man, as he was being dragged down to Hell by the skin of his face. The skin was being pulled down and off by a beastly, clawed hand reaching out from a crack within the ground, peeling their epidermis halfway down their face and revealing the skull that is bloodied, covered in red muscle tissue. The claws on the long, fur-covered fingers dug into the head, blood squirting and shooting out of everywhere. I can still remember the eyes bulging out of their sockets, the lines which are intricate made up the blood vessels in the eyeballs, every muscle mass fiber painted and extended so... accurately. The man's hand that's right out from underneath the ground, still struggling for freedom. It had been truly of good detail, very detail that is grotesque. It was too realistic. It nearly made me gag, the longer I looked at it.

I discovered there is more graffiti, each as gruesome was the next when I panned the light of my phone back down the alley. There was clearly certainly one of a woman being skinned alive by a figure that is shadowy a meat clever; there had been another of a man being stabbed with dozens of knives, as blood sprayed out of the wounds in visual information. There was even one of a woman in an purple that is old, hung upside-down, as a big saw came down between her legs, slicing her in two, as blood poured right out of the cut. I was beginning to feel sick, I pressed forward, plus the voices grew louder as I gagged at the sight of each "masterpiece," but. Thinking back it had been weird just how each of the disgusting pieces of 'art' was under a non-working light down the alley onto it, but.

I turned a large part in the back of the alley, peeked over the side of a dumpster, and spotted two figures that are darkened the shadows, standing in an area behind 2 or 3 structures. One man ended up being taller and skinnier. The tattered shirt that is white was wearing was old and ragged and had holes in it. He was not dressed for the elements, he was constantly scratching his left arm furiously and nervously as he shook and shivered to your cold, but. That made me think this man was an addict of some sort. He had all of the telltale signs of withdrawal. If his clothes didn't give that away, his sunken, bloodshot eyes and blackened crow's feet did. This man I saw obviously because of the one light that is working the alley, which was right above the 2 men. We never ever saw the other face that is man's. His back was to me personally, but his silhouette had been clear to see. He wore a heavy winter coating with a beanie that is thick-cut. He was shorter compared to the addict; if I had been to imagine, maybe five-foot-five, maybe five-foot-six. The taller man had been pleading to him, practically begging for one thing, probably a fix, but the faster, shadowy man was having none of it, as he just endured there silently. We clearly remember just what they stated.

"Come on, Joe, you know I'm good for it," the taller man pleaded in a hushed, whiney tone.

The shorter guy, this Joe guy, finally looked up you know the rules at him, but then shook their head, a puff of warm air escaping their lips, "I'm sorry, Jake. I gave you a to pay back the 500 bucks I lend you thirty days. That ran out yesterday month. Now, where's my money?"

From the Jake running his fingers through ear-length black hair you gotta think me before he said, "Look, Joe. It's been a month… that is slow"

But Joe wasn't having any of it. He cut Jake off that shit, Jake! Everybody knows you've been keeping a number of the item for yourself before he could spew another reason, "Don't give me. Just look you piece of shit at you! You look terrible."

"Please, Joe, you gotta believe me. Just provide me personally another chance."

I heard Joe inhale loudly, and saw their hand get as much as his face, as if to rub his eyes in annoyance. The memory is really so clear in my mind. I saw this "Joe" put your hands on their hips and once more shake his mind.

"I'm sorry, Jake, but you knew what happens to people who disappoint me, you pulled this shit anyhow, like the moron you might be. This season," Joe replied, as he raised a hand, removed a glove, and slowly, ever therefore slowly, reached for Jake for that, I'm afraid you won't be making it to Christmas.

Jake backed up from the wall, pleading, begging and yelling for Joe to stop. Oh, god, we still have nightmares about this part. In my dreams, I can still see the appearance of fear on Jake's face as Joe backed him against the wall surface. He was pleading for their life, and Joe just gave him… a shove that is gentle the chest? I was confused in the beginning by what I saw. Jake was afraid of a push that is slight? A shove that is gentle? I mean, that doesn't exactly sound like the most threatening of punishments, right? That ended up being what I thought before I saw Jake slip up a good five feet approximately, as if picked up by some force that is hidden. I stared as Jake shrilled and screamed, pinned from the wall surface. Only his head squirmed about.

Then I saw Jake break down right before my eyes, the single working light in the alley illuminating the ordeal that is whole. Jake had been turning into paint on the wall, bubbling and boiling as he screamed in anguish and pain. My heart sank into my stomach, and I also thought my eyes were planning to fallout, they felt therefore wide. The edges of Jake's silhouette boiled in what appeared to be multi-colored bubbles, as he sunk to the wall with a loud hiss of steam, like a hiss of a teapot that is boiling. I couldn't breathe; I just couldn't breathe, I never knew, become a painting on the wall surface, a literal damn painting on the wall surface when I saw Jake, a man.

The fear on his face immortalized for anybody to see within moments, Jake was simply a picture on the wall. Joe was peaceful, but large exhales of warm air burst down, as he raised his arm that is right to at the wall with his index finger. Joe then begun to move his hand counterclockwise in, if I remember correctly, circular motions. I ended up being so confused in the beginning as from what the hell was he doing, but to my surprise, Jake's human anatomy then began to move with Joe's hand. His human body began to spiral and twist around and around. Jake's face that is still screaming petrified with fear, elongated, as their body stretched more and more like chewed bubblegum. His body had become a stretched spiral; it was as as you would see in cartoons or science-fiction films if he was being sucked into a black opening. Finally, Joe seemed satisfied with his work, as Jake was absolutely nothing but a perfectly circular spiral of a person that is screaming. I simply stared on in horror and shock, as I viewed finished . that is entire.

In my state that is frightened slowly backed away, perhaps not thinking obviously, and that has been once I made the mistake of bumping over a trashcan. The sound that is crashing of against the floor snapped me personally out of my daze, when I looked down, startled, at the dropped trashcan before looking back up at Joe, who had been searching right at me. I nevertheless couldn't see his face. The light that is single the street obscured it from view. I could tell from the real way he stared me down with sick intent, however, that he did n't need any witnesses.

I endured there in stunned silence for a number of moments, as the two of us just stared at each other, waiting for the other to help make the move that is first. It was I quickly decided to make a run for it, sprinting down the street in exactly what felt like a blur. We could hear the fast footsteps of Joe right with every step behind me, slamming against the wet asphalt, splashing in puddles and gaining on me personally. Once I managed to make it to the entry of the alley, I looked to my left, maybe not wanting to lead Joe to my car, that was within the direction that is opposite. We been able to turn the street part and duck behind a motor vehicle before Joe could once again spot me. Staying close to the ground, we saw Joe dart past me personally and down the street in a pursuit that is blind. I sighed in relief, and once I was sure he had been gone, i obtained up from my hiding place, and hustled another two blocks down the sidewalk to my car. Finally, I ended up being safe... or therefore I thought. I understand that feels like a cliché, but it's a cliché that applies to just what took place next.

In a frantic and frenzy that is hurried I struggled to seize the automobile key and unlock my driver-side vehicle. My hands would stop shaking as n't I tried to slip the key into the lock. We hurried my means into the chair, fastening my seatbelt and slamming the entranceway whenever I finally managed. I was still in shock, as most of the fear – along with the realization of what had just occurred, and just what I'd witnessed – finally hit me all at once. Oh, god, I wanted to badly provide so, but we somehow managed to avoid that. I sat back in my seat and tried to get my breath. Some song that is stupid young ones liked arrived onto the radio; I just grunted and shut the damn thing off before I put the car in reverse.

Once we had backed fully away from the parking room, a man was noticed by me standing in the centre of the street through my back window.

It was Joe.

I became discovered by him.

Somehow, he fucking discovered me.

I panicked. I put the motor car in drive as fast as i really could and slammed the gas petal to the floor. I watched in my rearview mirror as Joe got further and further from sight, but he didn't try to give chase again. No, instead, he simply waved me off. He just slowly waved as I drove away down the street. It was thought by me odd, but i did son't really care. I was simply relieved that the experience ended up being over.

I raced all the real means home. We didn't worry about the speed limits; i simply wanted to go home where it had been safe. By the best time i arrived, it was 9 PM. My kids had been already asleep, and my wife was probably beginning her nightly ritual of reading some book that is random bed. Once parked into the driveway, I grabbed the bags from the backseat and marched to the door that is front unlocking it and tossing the bags onto the living room couch before hurrying to lock the door. I then hung my coat regarding the coat rack and trudged up the stairs to my bedroom. My spouse, sure sufficient, was currently in bed with her book, as I quietly entered the available space, took my clothes off, and headed to your bathroom to take a shower. I never heard my wife state such a thing like "Hey, honey, what's wrong?" or anything that way, and even I ended up being too scared and worn-out to control a reply if she had.

I carelessly discarded my clothes, trench layer and all sorts of, and immediately jumped into the shower. We didn't bother to do scrubbing that is much washing; I just needed to contemplate just what had just happened and figure things away. I thought about calling the authorities, but would they even trust me? No evidence was had by me of a murder, and I also knew individuals weren't going to believe me personally. Irrespective, after what felt like the longest shower in my own life, I dried myself off, put some pajamas on and slid into my bed close to my partner who by then had currently fallen asleep. We ensured to cuddle close to her as tightly me, making me feel safe for the first time that night as I could, permitting the warmth of her body engulf. It didn't take long before my eyelids got hefty, and I felt myself drift down to rest, feeling myself at comfort for enough time that is first exactly what felt like many years.

The morning that is next I woke up during intercourse alone. It was Saturday, so my partner together with children were most likely already up and about. My wife was probably downstairs making breakfast while the young kids were roughhousing, and as expected, these were. They certainly were heard by me clearly from the home. I sat up, looking over at the clock. It was 8:30 in the, being a Saturday, it was my day to check the mail because it usually came around 7:45 morning. Ah, routines, some semblance of normalcy weekend.

I got out of bed, place on my slippers and robe, and made my way downstairs. It had been then that the memories of the night that is previous flooding right back if you ask me. I paused halfway down the stairs, my heart skipping a beat, when I endured there in shock, staring at the discarded bags of my childrens' Christmas presents, carelessly strewn upon the living room couch. For a short moment i believed something terrible had happened, before the sounds originating from the kitchen area caught my attention again, pulling me back to comfort and reality. I walked down the stairs and looked over the railing to see my family, laughing and smiling around the table. I remember feeling a smile coming to my face, and I decided that, for their safety, I became simply going to forget about the before night.

I stepped away from the door that is front and also the cool air hit me personally hard, as I'd forgotten to connect my robe. I rolled my eyes in frustration and tied it before crossing the porch on my way to the steps that are front.

All those feelings being sappy along with any hope of forgetting the events through the night before, had been dashed immediately once I reached the top the actions. In the walkway ultimately causing my mailbox, a message was noticed by me scrawled across it in red spray paint. The fear and surprise returned, as I felt my heart sink into my belly. What the message said continues to haunt me to this day that is very. Just five simple, everyday terms have turned my life completely on its head. It read:

I TRULY LIKE YOUR HOUSE.

Merry Christmas,

From: Joe

I looked down in horror. A glimmer of light hit my eyes, I noticed something different, taped to the gatepost as it was then. We walked over and examined it. It was a Polaroid image of a grouped family sitting yourself down to breakfast.

My loved ones.

I turned to look over the screen, and there they were, smiling and sitting as they had been within the picture, without a care in the globe.

But so was Joe.

His form that is shadowy loomed the window, waving if you ask me like he did the night before. Oh, god… he's in my house. I led him to the house!

A PRETTY PAPER

One contrary wheel wobbled erratically as Thomas Moon pushed against the shopping cart application that is weighted. He looked down during the hill of Christmas presents and imagined his wallet that is bad gasping air and fainting in a huff. He smiled as his spouse, Christine, waddled up to the cart carrying what seemed to be sufficient rolls of wrapping paper to cover roughly two and a half football industries.

"You yes that's enough paper?" he asked, mockingly. "There might be a trees that are few in the rainforest."

"Hardy-har," she replied, a grin that is lopsided across her face. She stuffed the paper that is wrapping into the overburdened cart and leaned near to her husband's ear.

"Keep speaking, funny man,you might not get your special Christmas gift" she whispered, "And. One I got at that store that is little the mall. You know, the one that offers dozens of lacy, skimpy things?"

"And shutting up now," said Thomas, with a large, toothy grin. "And merry Christmas to me."

"I think this is everything," said Christine. "No, wait. We haven't gotten my mother anything yet."

"How about a solution that is first-class the North Pole?" replied Thomas.

"I thought you had been shutting up," said Christine. "Be nice when we go over to my parents."

"I'm always nice," said Thomas, "but your mother hates me personally."

"She does not hate you," said Christine.

"The girl begged you to not marry me," he responded. Day"On our wedding. In the church."

"I remember, I remember," she said. "But that was 10 years ago."

"And she nevertheless hates me," responded Thomas. "I've never ever been good enough."

"Well, duh," said Christine, jokingly. "After all, i'm the princess that is high settled for a dirty commoner far beneath her station."

Thomas swept her up into his hands.

"Oh, when we get home I'm going to show you simply how dirty this commoner are."

She kissed him and whispered into his ear, "Who says we're waiting until we get home?"

"What?" he asked.

She replied, nevertheless whispering, "You're going to wheel this buggy towards the checkout line while we go obtain the crockpot my mom has been hinting at for six months. Then we're parking somewhere out of the real way and you're fucking my brains out in the backseat like we're horny teenagers. Understood?"

"Yes, ma'am," he replied, using down for the front associated with the store like he'd won a shopping that is timed and also the clock was almost up.

Getting everything into the rear of the SUV was like playing a game that is high-level of. After loading and unloading and reloading, twisting and turning and stacking the relative back gate finally closed and latched. Just the wrapping paper rolls remained in the cart and Christine slid them onto the seat that has returned.

Thomas pulled off onto the dark, dead-end side road. The wrapping paper ended up being precariously balanced on the mound of presents in the rear as Christine balanced herself atop Thomas in the seat that is right back. Fundamentally, as the SUV began to rock, the rolls of paper toppled onto them in a shower of silver bells, red-nosed reindeer, green wreaths and white snowmen.

* * * * * *

Jeffrey, eight years of age, and his bro Michael, also eight years of age (although he claimed eldest by seventeen minutes), scooped the last two handfuls of snow onto the ball of their snowman's head. Michael took two shiny, semi-circular rocks he had dug from beneath the snowfall atop the driveway and pressed them into the mind. Jeffrey shoved in a pilfered-from-the-fridge carrot just underneath them.

"You think Santa will bring us some brand new games?" Jeffrey asked his brother.

"Paulie Jenkins says Santa isn't real," replied Michael.

"Paulie Jenkins can't even tie his shoes that are own" said Jeffrey. "He's real. Mother and Dad say therefore."

"Maybe," said Michael. "I'm gonna find out."

"How?" asked Jeffrey.

"Tonight, after Mom and Dad go to sleep," began Michael, "I'm gonna sneak back downstairs. I'm gonna wait up and see."

"You're gonna make Santa mad," said Jeffrey. "He's not gonna leave you anything."

"We'll see," replied Michael.

"You'll see," said Jeffrey. "I'm not taking the chance."

"Fine, you baby that is big" said Michael.

"I might be an infant," replied Jeffrey, "but I'll be a baby with Christmas presents."

"Boys!"

The two brothers switched towards the homely house since the screen door squeaked open and Christine's voice echoed throughout the yard. "Time to come in!"

The stockings were hung by the five-brick, wall-hanging gasoline heater with care, the tree lights were on and the cookies and milk had been half gone so it looked like Santa had simply been there. Thomas placed the gift that is final the tree and stepped straight back. He looked out across the shimmering sea of bright, multicolored paper bathed in the dull light for the Christmas tree.

He smiled because the designs printed on the paper brought back sweet back seat memories. He closed his eyes, imagining the curve of Christine's breasts because they bounced in the moonlight that is dim.

"All done?" Christine asked quietly, breaking the spell of memory.

"Just put down the last one," he replied, his voice low to help keep from waking Jeffrey and Michael.

"Let's hit the sack," she said. "I'm exhausted and the boys will early be up."

"No special Christmas present?" he asked, making sad puppy eyes.

"Not tonight," she said. Night"Tomorrow. After every one of the madness is over."

"I'm holding you to that," he said.

Michael sat up during sex as he heard his parents' door close. He itched to spring from the bed and rush down the stairs but he stopped himself. He looked over at Jeffrey, sound asleep, a line that is thin of creeping from his mouth and dampening their pillow.

Michael thought of waking him but decided against it. Let him rely on stupid Santa that is old if wanted. Michael waited fifteen mins. He hoped that was long enough to make yes his parents were during sex and maybe even asleep. He then slipped from his sleep and tiptoed across the space. The bedroom door creaked it and he grimaced as he exposed. Michael looked back. Jeffrey was still drooling on their pillow. Michael made their way down the hall, past his parents' room near the top of the stairs. He crept down, praying the stairs would remain silent and not creak.

He breathed a sigh of relief as he stepped silently away from the stair that is last into the living room. He smiled joyfully at the sight of the presents beneath the tree. They seemed to fill half the space. His eyes scanned across them, then stopped within the middle. Michael did not understand why, but his heart beat faster. The air around him seemed to chill and goose pimples broke out over their skin.

It absolutely was just a box, and Michael couldn't explain why looking him have the way it did at it made. The box endured out amongst the other gift suggestions, as it was wrapped like no other gift underneath the tree. In which the paper adorning the other gifts were colored mottled and bright because of the hieroglyphs of Christmas time, this paper had been jet black. A black so deep it did actually swallow, instead of exhibit, the dim light that is colored by the Christmas tree bulbs. The box ended up being around three feet tall and a ribbon that is red around the sides and came together in a bow on the top. Micheal had never seen a so... that is red. well, red. That ended up being the way in which that is only brain could explain it.

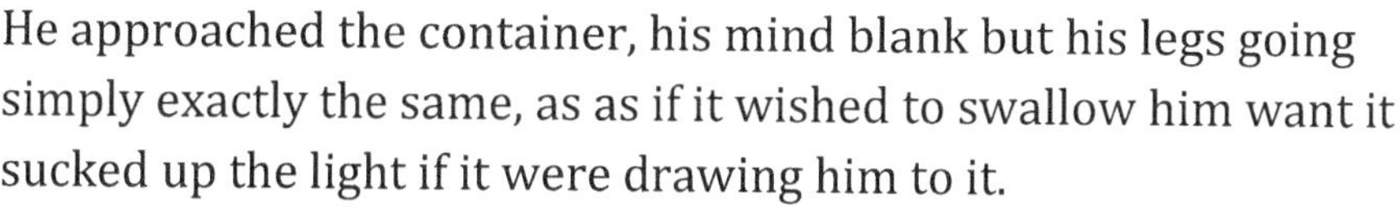

He approached the container, his mind blank but his legs going simply exactly the same, as as if it wished to swallow him want it sucked up the light if it were drawing him to it.

And then it did.

Thomas awoke with a jerk. He could have sworn he heard one thing, something that sounded like one the guys had started crying out, and then stopped suddenly. He glanced at the clock. 1:00 AM. Christine stirred beside him.

"Whats'amatter?" she mumbled.

"Think the boys may be up," he said softly.

"A'ready?" she replied, still half-asleep.

"Heard something downstairs," he stated.

"Alright," she said, shaking the sleep from her mind. "Might as well obtain it over with."

"I guess," he said. "We can always get back to bed." They pulled by themselves from beneath their covers that are warm slipped on housecoats and slippers, and made their way downstairs.

"Guess I was wrong," said Thomas. He searched the available room with their eyes but found no trace of the boys.

"Guess so," said Christine. "Wait, what is that?" She pointed towards the gifts.

Thomas looked at the box. "What?" he said. "It's just a gift."

"I didn't buy any wrapping that is black, did you?"

"No," he replied. It dawned on him that the present wasn't familiar. Every present had been placed by him underneath the tree really. All except any particular one.

"Where did which come from?" he asked.

Christine did answer that is n't. She was approaching the gift that is dark her human anatomy stiff, arm outstretched, almost just as if she were entranced. And then it was touched by her.

Christine squealed because the gift was moved by her and Thomas rushed to her side. He stopped in surprise.

Christine's hand had sunk into the paper that is dark. She tried to pull away however the present pulled back, dragging her arm in as if it were a pit of tar. Thomas grabbed his wife and pulled, but the darkness dragged her ever deeper. Then, with an strength that is unnatural something on the other part pulled them both into the blackness.

* * * * * *

Thomas thought it was one of the strangest dreams he'd ever had. He then opened his eyes and wondered why he was lying in snowfall. Had he been sleepwalking? Why wasn't he colder? He sat up and wondered if he was still dreaming. Snow covered the ground as far as he could see. Which was pretty much all he could see. Darkness surrounded him and stretched in to the distance.

"It's perhaps not a dream, you know," arrived a sound from behind him. Thomas looked toward the vocals and then scrambled to his feet to back away from its owner.

The person, if the expressed term applied, ended up being short. Just maybe five feet high. He had been wearing a fur that is red the color of dried blood. It ended up being ragged and dirty and reached to the knee. Brown pants adorned the feet, also dirty, and moth-eaten. Its feet, hands and face were uncovered, but a pointed cap that is red atop its head, dirty whilst the rest of the ensemble. It was the actual face that made Thomas recoil.

Its epidermis had been scabrous and wrinkled, the color of old pus. The skin regarding the tactile hands and feet matched. The lined face held two eyes that are bloodshot the pupils dark as soot. Its nose had been long and curved down to a true point as razor-sharp as a razor. The ears were long and pointed. The hand and toenails had been claw-like and long.

"I-I'm still asleep," muttered Thomas.

"Didn't you hear me?" said the creature before him. "It's not a dream. Someone's been sexy. Very naughty. We can smell your sins. I could taste them in the air. A dream? No, no. Allow me to prove it to you."

Then your creature was gone just as if it had been never there. The hairs on Thomas's body stood up straight as he felt breath that is hot his neck. He screamed as sharp teeth sank into his shoulder and pulled back from a wet smack to his flesh.

"Still think you're dreaming?" asked the creature, it is mouth wet with blood.

"W-What do you w-want?" asked Thomas, "W-w-where am I?" He gripped their wounded shoulder.

"You're where most of the naughty guys that are little girls go," said the creature. "You're where they come with regards to their punishments. And, oh, what sights i must show you!"

The creature laughed, a cackle that is long. A light that is bright Thomas and instantly he had been someplace else.

a vehicle. His car. No, his old automobile. The one he had in college. His Mustang. Thomas had been behind the wheel, foot regarding the gasoline. He tried to take it down and hit the breaks but he couldn't. It was like his foot was welded to the pedal.

"Nice car," arrived a voice from the seat that has returned. Thomas looked around see the creature smiling to the rearview mirror.

"I've lost my mind," said Thomas.

"You wish," replied the creature. "Lost a lot in this ride, didn't you? Lost your virginity back here in this chair that is back. Lost the pocket knife your father gave you between the seats. Never did believe it is, did you? Funny, such things as that. So close, but so difficult to find. Remember why you ditched this ride, Tommy boy?"

"I... I... no," stammered Thomas.

"Well, possibly this will refresh your memory," said the creature, pointing out of the windshield.

The kid was twelve years old. Riding his bike at night. No reflectors. Thomas tried and screamed in vain to remove his base from the accelerator as the bike crunched beneath the wheels therefore the boy rolled up the bonnet and across the windshield, spider webs of cracks tracing their course. Thomas heard the sickening, wet thunk as the boy impacted the pavement behind him.

"Not gonna stop?" asked the creature. "Just like in those days, huh? Nothing like good hit-and-run that is old make the bloodstream pump, right, Tommy boy?"

Tears streamed down his face as Tommy said, "No, no, no, no, please, I was just a kid, simply a kid that is frightened. It wasn't my fault. I didn't see him."

"Oh, yeah," stated the creature. "It wasn't your fault at all. It was all that bottle of whiskey and that rail of blow that did it, right?"

"Please," begged Thomas as he stared through the windshield. His heart froze as he saw more individuals within the road. Three people in the exact distance and rapidly growing closer. He attempted to steer away from their website but their hands were as trapped as his base. He screamed as the three people linked aided by the car. He screamed so loud their voice broke as these people were recognized by him. Jeffrey spun from the side of the automobile to be kept a heap that is broken the medial side of the trail. Thomas felt Michael pass beneath the wheels with a thump that is damp. Christine rolled up the bonnet and smashed headfirst through the windshield. Her mind hung through the opening, bloodstream dripping from her auburn that is long hair. Thomas squeezed his eyes sobbed and shut.

When he opened their eyes once again, the engine car ended up being gone. He now sat at his desk at work. He glanced around at the cubicles that are empty. Very nearly empty. Some body stood three cubicles down. He knew that cubicle too well.

"Oh, yes you do," came the voice that is creature's. Had Thomas spoken out loud, or had the creature read his brain? At this point, Thomas did care that is n't. He just wanted the nightmare to finish. He looked towards the voice. The creature had changed. The gnarled, yellowish face protruded from the wall, clock hands sticking from the sides of the nose that is crooked. Fleshy numbers surrounded the face.

"You remember this," said the creature, "this fantasy come true. evening"

As the occupant was spoken by the creature of the cubicle three cubicles down made her way down the aisle.

"Norma," said Thomas, his voice dry and harsh.

"Hmmm, lovely Norma," said the creature, she tasted"Do you remember how? The sounds she made? The desk that is broken you lied planning to get replaced?"

Norma stood before him, locks red as fire and a physical body that should have been hot to the touch. She bent and kissed him, just they certainly were the only ones left in the office as she had that night when. But this right time had been various. He remembered the kiss as sweet and warm, but this right time her tongue forced its method into his mouth. The tongue was slimy and pointed. And didn't stop. He gagged as it slid down his throat further than any tongue that is individual perhaps go. He heaved and coughed when she finally pulled back. He attempted to rise from their seat but couldn't, trapped once more.

Norma hiked her skirt up around her waist and lifted herself up onto the desk.

Again, things were a caricature that is sick of Thomas remembered. The thin landing that is red of hair above her mound was the same, but that was all. Below it was a gaping, tooth-filled maw. Thomas tried to pull back as not-Norma wrapped her legs over their shoulders and pulled him closer. He screamed again whilst the teeth ripped into their face, then his neck after they had torn away his jaw. His last sound was a gurgle that is bloody the muscle tissue of his heart ruptured.

The creature shuddered in near-orgasmic glee.

* * * * * *

Christine remembered blackness, and snow so far as the eye could then see waking up at the clinic. A dream, she told herself.

She hadn't told Thomas. She had made the appointment, talked to your professionals, and now here she was, waiting the hours that are few the dilator sticks called laminaria to slowly stretch her cervix available. They didn't need another child, she told herself. Thomas would agree. They had both always been pro-choice. Then why hadn't he had been told by her?

"Why indeed?" asked the medical practitioner.

"What?" asked Christine, looking at the physician. A double-take was done by her. This wasn't the doctor who performed her procedure. Performed. Past-tense, thought Christine. What's happening?

"Someone's a liar," said the doctor, pulling straight down their mask to reveal a yellowish, hideous face. "That's what's going on."

"Who are you?" Christine screamed. "What do you want?"

"Your husband asked the same," said the creature.

"Thomas?" she asked. "What have you done with Thomas?"

"Oh, Thomas is a bit beneath the weather," said the creature, wanting to hold back a laugh that is vicious. "Something he consumed."

Christine attempted to move but couldn't. She was strapped towards the table, her legs up in stirrups. "Please just let me get, or perhaps tell me what you want, please."

"What do i would like?" asked the creature, "What do I wish with my of freedom night? Why, you're currently giving me personally everything I want. Your pain, your fear, your sin. It's all so…. delicious."

Christine had started to cry.

"Please," she said, "I have kiddies. Please, just I want to go."

"Oh, I know," said the creature. "The young ones, sins therefore sweet, yet so few. So time that is little be nasty. Mostly innocent. Like their mother. So few genuine, juicy sins. Not like your husband. A couple was had by him whoppers."

"What are you currently discussing?" she asked through tears.

"Oh, you didn't know, of program," said the creature, "not about the murder...."

"M-murder?"

"Hmmm, yes, hit-and-run," said the creature. "Little boy, not much more than your guys. Back in his school days. You were dating then. You remember his Mustang? That night he drove up with a battered and bloody front side end?"

"No," she said. "That...w as a deer. A deer was struck by him."

The creature laughed. "No," it said. "He went down a boy that is little. And then he drove to your house, all weepy and in shock and said it was a deer, and do you remember what you did? It had been so sexy that he had been all separated about a deer? the method that you thought"

"No, please, just…" she said. "Please."

"How does it feel knowing the very first time you fucked your would-be husband, he had just killed just a little child?"

"I…" Christine started, but her voice broke into a scream as pain ripped through her.

"And, of program, you didn't know about the affair, did you? No clue your husband came home and kissed you after burying his face between another woman's legs? We wonder, did he even shower after bending her over his desk and over your bed? before he bent you"

Christine sobbed as pain wracked through her.

"Well, well, " said the creature, "guess it's time we got this baby out of you, eh?"

Christine screamed again. It felt like something large – something too big to be inside her – was ripping its solution of her. She slumped, sweat covered, as whatever it was finally kept her body.

She handled to lift her head because the creature approached, a large, blanket-wrapped bundle in his hands. It's nails that are dirty during the blanket, pulling it aside.

Michael's face peeked through the bundle. Christine screamed as she looked at her son, screamed therefore very long her voice broke and died into a croak that is near-soundless.

Michael's face ended up being gaunt, dry and thin, as if all that made the boy alive had been drawn out. His eyes were milky orbs that are white. Teeth were visible behind his lips that are cracked. The gums had pulled away them loose and bloody from them, making. The jaw that is desiccated.

"Mom?" he asked, their voice like rustling leaves. Your skin of Michael's face cracked since it moved.

"Little Mikey here ended up being the first to touch my field," said the creature. "I sucked him dry, what little there was. A lie that is white, a brotherly punch there."

Christine attempted to talk but could find no terms. Hot tears streamed down her cheeks and her jaw worked up and down, useless.

Michael tried to speak once again, to ask he did the cracks in his face spread for her again, however when. They stretched out like shattering glass and Christine finally found another scream her son wither and crumble to dust as she viewed. Whilst the last of Michael sifted between the hands which can be creature's Christine's head broke into pieces and blew away.

* * * * * *

Jeffrey pulled himself out from under his bed covers and hit the floor operating. He slid to a stop at the doorway and glanced at his brother's bed. Empty. He ran down the hallway to his parents' room and pushed available the door. Another bed that is empty. He ran down the stairs, that he was never, ever supposed to operate on the stairs though he knew. The sun crept through the living room windows, the light dancing off the gift place that is colored. He stopped, searching the available room for his household. There is no one, simply piles of gifts. He expected noise, laughter, the odor of his parents breakfast that is making. There was nothing. No smell of coffee and bacon, no sound of a brother's Christmas that is joyous morn. He looked again at the gift ideas, two piles on each relative part of the tree as well as in the middle... nothing. Just a void, big enough for a box to be.

Jeffrey's heart began to beat hard, fear running up his body.

"Dad?" he called out. "Mom?"

SOLE SURVIVOR HUMAN

He was cool. Bitterly so. It wasn't the unforgiving December wind creating lazy vortexes in the freshly falling snow; rather, it was the numbness that ingested both body and heart in one fatal, unseen breeze. It additionally didn't escape him that their surroundings seemingly felt the same: deserted and bleak.

Perhaps deserted wasn't the expression that is proper. Being two times before Christmas, there were individuals who are numerous the cityscape. Some gathered under building awnings for shelter; others slumped inside their cars locked bumper to bumper; and still others reclined upon street benches, awaiting public transportation that will come never ever. Perhaps the physical systems sprawled awkwardly here and there in the street as well as on the sidewalk testified this town had not been deserted. No birds perched in rotting trees which arched to your sky that is darkened no Christmas shoppers hustled and bustled for last-minute gifts, no children warred along with other kiddies in the time-honored battle for snowball superiority. Dead.

A condemning chill raced i'm alone through him with the speed of thought.

However, it absolutely was not his exposure that is very first to.

For the ten years that is past he had invested his existence secluded in the beautifully barren confines of a Canadian parcel of land into the Arctic Circle. The temperatures that are sub-zero of little concern; in reality, the serrated blades of arctic wind refreshed and strengthened him. Curiously, this environment inspired their survival that is proceeded and him safe in an Arctic embrace. Although the prospect of durability outweighed the void of companionship in his early years, their later years were a test that's true of in solitude.

Periodically, the man that is old go to him, briefly dispersing the looming shade of lethal monotony. The old man's eyes forever sparkled with an hope that is eternal constantly, providing a jovial laugh with any story, suspending the soulless sorrow of isolation. Regrettably, that cheer could not prevent the predator of loneliness from eagerly coming back shortly after the old man departed, on their solution to whatever brought him away from his happy home into the place that is first.

In those full days without the convenience of some other, he'd curse the warmth of friends, trying unsuccessfully to deny he even needed companionship. Yet, deep down, he knew he would instantly return to civilization in a heartbeat. Nonetheless, he knew he could perhaps not return, as the enemy would be waiting. And the enemy would not just take pity on him.

His nemesis had been far from omniscient, nevertheless the Beast will not need to be. Their foe had spread its influence all about countries, cities, and suburbs like a virulent plague. No one could conceal from the Beast in these places. The enemy did have a weakness; a period of time that is brief of every year. Yet, he nevertheless felt unsure as to the Beast's machinations as those durations were not easily calculated, it safe against the enemy with the deadly look and kept to your safety of their frozen sanctuary so he played.

He had perhaps not forgotten that terrifying encounter that is first. He remembered the incident with crystal-clear accuracy, burned into him like a glowing branding iron kissing flesh that is virgin. The had sleepily awakened when the enemy assaulted with sadistic fury morning. Their human anatomy had become a well of pain under the Beast's talons that are well-honed feeling as if millions of razor blades ripped into him. Every pore screamed, yet the Beast drank easily from their essence, one excruciating sip at the same time. He felt the scoffing eyes of the enemy toying with him, as if to express 'the worst is yet to come!' He knew further hellacious torments awaited him if he did not immediately retreat. Wracked with deep pain, he fled to your outer reaches of northern Canada, a accepted destination where his nemesis did not follow. Possibly it was the extreme conditions or the geography; however, the enemy had, in one stroke that is ironic condemned him to this frigid tundra and spared him.

But now he endured defiantly into the world of his nemesis, fearless of retaliation. The enemy had been put in check, and it had been known by him.

The crux of the conflict occurred months prior, in the night time sky that is deep. Movie stars seductively winked he watched the glorious beauty of this Northern Lights swaying in heaven's inky darkness at him as. He then noticed a object that is strange from the sky. A meteorite? An space satellite that is old? Whatever the truth, the item maintained a nature that is purposeful. It absolutely was then that a second, then a third, then a meteorite that is fourth; they did actually multiply exponentially. The meteorites gashed the sky that is serene the stars retreated under the onslaught of hundreds of projectiles. Repulsed, he turned away from the aerial horde, only discover a mirror of the same regarding the horizon that is opposite. Seemingly ignorant of each other, the projectiles laced between one another. Most sped off to their destination unmolested. But, periodically, some would cross paths issuing an eruption of brutal luminescence. It absolutely was he then discovered the bright, explosive flashes were missiles. Nuclear missiles. He could not bear to watch the horror, and retreated to the confines of his igloo.

It had been like resting through a distant thunderstorm as the mechanical abominations rumbled throughout the atmosphere with small flashes like violent, destructive heat lightning.

He noticed the sky; or in other words, the lack of it when he left his igloo much later on. In its place was a dirty film that is gray of, thick and smothering. The nuclear bombs had tossed the waste of their destruction into the environment, defying the movie stars to shine or even a satellite to broadcast an Emergency that is crucial Broadcasting message down on the planet. The Earth had become a coffin that is lightless an ecological nightmare as a casket lid. He guessed that what the nukes didn't vaporize, or rays didn't kill, the environment that is polluted handily finish down.

Weeks later, a vocals was heard by him at his door: "Anybody home?" It was the weakened voice of the man that is old.

He stared with a combination of sympathy and revulsion whenever he laid his dark eyes upon the old man. Radiation had taken control of the old human body that is man's. Putrid facial lesions had been painfully visible and large patches of now-hairless parts of their head had been replaced by wet, runny, red splotches. Thick mucus that is green saliva went unchecked through the old man's nose and lips, and the old man's swollen, irradiated hands were as red and puffy since the parka he wore.

"Just thought I'd stop by for a visit." The old man tried to chuckle, which converted into a bout of wracking, painful coughing. The light was fading fast. "Well, my kid, also it doesn't do me personally much good though I know who's been naughty. The Earth is dying, my boy. I'm pretty wily, but," the man that is old at the bloody holes in his fingers where nails when grew, "even I'm maybe not immune. Matter of fact, my pack that is last animal away 'bout a half-mile from here. Poor Don, he attempted, but the fight is taken by those nukes out of you." Tears welled and ran down the man's that is old cheeks.

"Please, you can't-"

"Don't begin on me personally," the man that is old in. "We all gotta go some time. Just never thought we'd all go at enough time that is same. We're all dead, my boy. Every animal and plant. Dead or dying. 'Cept you." The man that is old to the floor of the igloo, hacking blood and lung tissue. He cradled the man that is old he continued to hack. "God, how I pity you. You'll survive. I recently age slow, however you..." Another series of coughs shook the man's frame that is old. "So... sorry..." the old guy sputtered, before a violent death rattle extinguished the remaining fire from their eyes.

Now, him, he reflected on people who offered him life as he stood in the silence and gray soot associated with Midwestern town that spawned. His makers knew very little of the arts that are arcane yet, caught in the throes of creativity, these youthful wizards had used base alchemy and typical elements to provide him life.

Was it, he thought, a device that is magical? My creators' desire? Fate? Hand of God? Frankly, he would not have the reasoning capability to properly analyze such an subject that is esoteric nor did he care to dwell long on it.

The most memory that is vivid had was for the day the Beast had forced him to go out of. He had been waving farewell to a lady that is little a fluffy pink winter layer and dense white corduroy pants. He could see she ended up being fighting the movement of tears and a heart that is hefty. She waved back with a hand that is mittened.

He called back to her. "I'll be back again someday."Don't you cry,""

Now, he had returned. Perhaps not it mattered anymore. The young girl in the pink wintertime coating ended up being surely a dead, frozen husk. Like the remainder of humanity. Like the animals. Just like the plants and flowers. Like every thing that is living planet Earth.

Except for him.

He walked through the snowfall that is dirty stopping during the city square. Amidst the dead and discarded machinery of mankind stood the town's wilted Christmas tree, decked with bold ornaments and garland that is shimmering. Despite the fact that Christmas was simply two days away, he did not feel celebratory. Every ounce of Christmas character drained from him the moment Santa Claus died in his hands someplace in the harsh Canadian North in a igloo that is desolate.

The survivor that is sole of started initially to weep, for he knew his nemesis, the Beast referred to as Sun, would not appear again for many, many decades. That is, if he was lucky, or fate was merciful. The golem of snow once called Frosty continued walking without location. Black tears flowed unchecked from eyes made out of coal. And his tears were cool. Bitterly so.

KEEP STAY OF THE ICE

From the time grade three, my friends and i possibly could make Derek Zimmer believe any such thing. Anything. From Pop-Rocks and Coke will make your stomach explode; to earwigs actually burrow in your ears (and one's on your shoulder at this time!); to the typical legend that is urban of babysitter therefore the killer upstairs – and that it actually occurred to someone in our neighborhood.

The prank that is most readily useful we pulled on Derek must be in grade 6, whenever we told him that every person had to go into the girl's bathroom to alter because a toilet had overflowed within the boy's. This had been during gym class too and in our school, the bathrooms doubled as change rooms. Geez, he didn't even question it – didn't even wait to see us go in first. We followed right him carrying their spare set of clothes, a towel over their shoulder behind him. We didn't even need to shove him in; he just walked through the hinged door and we locked it behind him and from then on there is nothing but hollering and shrieking from one other side. I got to admit, We still get tickled thinking about it.

After grade seven it stopped being– that is funny pulling ones on him on a regular basis. But, like a practice that is bad we kept feeding him lies and watching him fall for them again and again.

I guess it didn't help that he had sheltering, hovercraft parents. I suggest, the guy believed in Santa Clause until he ended up being thirteen, for God's sake! And so they kept walking him to school even though he lived literally just up the road. It wasn't until Derek begged them, after being tortured by our sneers and jeers, that they finally stopped.

You'd think by teaching him perhaps not to think everything he was told that they'd have tried to protect him. But i suppose simply because they did everything for him, he just always required someone else to make his mind up.

I don't want you to have the impression that Derek was slow or something. He was really a pretty kid that is bright. He was top that is n't of class or nothing – and his math and science marks were pathetically low. But, with him, you'd see he was really very insightful, particularly when it arrived to abstract stuff like morality and friendship and artsy stuff too if you spent time. Oh yes, I happened to be friends with Derek, also though we constantly made and tricked fun of him. Yeah…I was one of those friends. He would actually analyze our favorite television shows, comparing the ones he liked and those he didn't and get into really detail that is meticulous why some were good, plus some were bad. Just what made a tale funny and just what didn't.

During the time, despite having him, I sort of thought that most this information was pretty useless – I mean, I just viewed shows, movies and played video games for fun, not to ever write a goddamn dissertation though we liked chatting! If Derek had any brains, I thought, he'd put more of their energy into his schoolwork. Nevertheless now, searching straight back, it creates me wish our school had a Philosophy class as well as an creative arts system. I believe he'd have excelled, in the place of constantly being stuck C's that is getting and. But we grew up in a small, frozen town in northern Ontario that only offered the bare necessities for a diploma. And in a town where most people work in the mines and spend their spare time ice-fishing or playing hockey, Derek stuck out like a thumb that is sore.

All the trained teachers seemed to like him, but you could inform they were pretty aggravated by how difficult he found the material. He was additionally a bit stubborn often times. As an example, you'd think he would have done well in English, right? Wrong. He shined only within the writing that is creative but didn't follow instructions and would never read the publications that were assigned. The funny thing was, he ended up being a voracious reader, always reading something. He just didn't desire to be bothered Lord that is reading of Flies or Of Mice and Men. He just thought they certainly were a waste of his time.

Something that Derek excelled at, besides being a very buddy that is loyal to a fault – was storytelling. Him, he'd tell it in a way that we would hold on every word he said when he got an urban legend, or a dirty joke, or if something occurred to. There was no rambling, no "um's" or "uh's" – he always took his some time told the entire tale completely. The punchline or the ending of his story had been always left and clear us howling with laughter, terrified, or desperate to hear more.

Many of this whole stories Derek told us had been uncannily frightening – tales of ghosts and animals inside our very own hometown. A lot of them i really could trace back to some origin – usually Alvin Schwartz's Scary Stories to inform in the Dark. But there were also a few I had never been aware of and may perhaps not find a source for. Him using this, he would give me this knowing smile, their light eyes at ease, and state, "There are somethings that can't be explained. whenever we confronted" He would then pontificate about the other world and how everyone was able to access it if they just suspended their prejudices and disbelief. That has been how he got "beamed" his stories, he had said. During the right time, I thought it ended up being bullshit. This was the matter that is only had ever known Derek to lie about. Now looking straight back, I desire I had realized that this truthful, gullible boy ended up being incompetent at telling falsehoods. And that what I had been being told by him was something he at minimum considered to be real.

Eventually, I got a bit jealous of Derek; I never had a memory that is great details – apart from numbers and figures – and often when I told a joke, I'd forget a significant part for the set-up and also the punchline would fall flat. Or that i thought was funny or exciting, after I'd finish, the listeners would just stare blankly, their vacant faces tacitly screaming, "That's it? if I told an anecdote about a thing that happened to me"

(trust in me, it took me a time that is long a lot of effort to create this story in addition to I have).

I was also jealous of Derek because of the attention he got from girls. He had been tall, fit and good-looking although he had beenn't very athletic. And his nature that is gullible think, made many of them think he was sweet. You realize, like a lost puppy you need to be careful of. Regrettably for them, Derek was too absorbed in his world that is own of comic books, Stephen King, Family Guy, and Doctor whom to ever take a hint.

This got really interesting in grade ten when Christie Blackwell, a girl that is preppy the states, came to our town. Her family members was from Montana and her daddy had come here for a few work that is administrative local the mining company. We didn't know it during the right time, but their place and his family members's move were only temporary.

Now, we had nothing that is likely normal with this woman, but both Derek and I were absolutely smitten. We guess every person was pretty fascinated by this new, pretty face from somewhere exotic – like Montana when you're in a small town all of the kids date each other's sisters and exes, so.

For a weeks being few she was all Derek and i possibly could talk about. A number of our other friends thought she was cute too, but Derek and I had been head-over-heels. I, however, never got up the courage to speak with her. I would are top of my class and on the lacrosse team but, I knew the things I was into the eyes of girls – a short, fat, sarcastic little child with a disposition that is sour. Derek, but, he didn't have the cowardice that is same had. He actually went as much as her lunch that is during break talked with her!

He was watched by me approach, grinning from ear to ear, awaiting the humiliation therefore the peal of shrieking laughter from the other girls. But – she really chatted with him. She was favorably radiant as he introduced himself and I also was going to have a heart assault when – she invited him to take a seat at her table– I thought.

I'll admit, I had been enraged. It wasn't fair. It just. Wasn't. Fair. For some idiot like Derek, with no prospects for future years, to own that girl. And what would that mean for me personally? Why would he wish to loaf around some loser whenever that girl had been had by him on his arm?

Luckily, Derek – as I've said – didn't just take hints easily, that he finally had been ready to ask her out so that it wasn't until a rumor had started about her liking him.

Of course, I was told by him first.

Night"Jimmy!" he shouted over the phone one. I recall I actually winced from the receiver. "Guess what?" his voice blared at arm's length. After putting the phone back once again to my ear, I asked him, and he told me from one regarding the girls that Christie liked him that he had heard it.

A stone was felt by me form within the pit of my stomach. Don't misunderstand me, I knew that i'dn't have gotten Christie. I recently thought neither of us would. So, the actual fact her, and I hadn't, really burned my ass which he got.

But then, a concept had been got by me. an idea that would haunt me personally for the rest of my life.

"Derek," I said to the phone. "She doesn't actually as you. I overheard her and Jennifer (the girl who told him). They're just playing a trick on you."

There clearly was silence on the other end.

Derek mumbled out a"But... that is pitiful and I knew I'd to pounce.

"Listen," we implored, "if you ask Christie away on a night out together, everybody else will just laugh at you. They're just doing this to produce a fool out of you right in front of everyone."

Again, silence fell in the other end. I could then visualize Derek with their head hanging down, all mopey like he sometimes got.

Then, it was taken by me a little further. Over the line.

"I mean, c'mon, consider it. You and her? She's just been within our school three weeks and she's already top of the class.

Everyone else turns their mind to see her. Exactly how have you been likely to enough be good for that?"

I felt that stone in the pit of my stomach once more, but this time for yet another reason, after hearing Derek sadly mumble, "You're right…"

Shamelessly, we changed the subject, asking him if we were going to still go out this to play X-box at his house but, his sound never came back to normal week-end.

That, I barely slept evening. I truly felt like shit.

This was the key that is first pulled on Derek that made me feel like that. But it wouldn't function as the last.

It absolutely was grade eleven, when Lloyd (our other friend) and the pranks were taken by me personally past an acceptable limit.

Lloyd and I also had simply gotten back our exam results for grade 11 Physics and, while we didn't fail, these marks weren't going to appear good on a university application either. Plus, it was December, so there was time that is n't much in the semester to replace with it. Of course, ole Derek wasn't in Physics. Or Chemistry. Or Biology. Some loophole had been found by him in a technicality to just take something called "Earth and Space Science" in grade 12 for his science/technology credit (don't ask me how the Ontario education system works).

Additionally, around this time, Derek was getting super-obsessed with comic books and writing his own (report cards and prospects that are postsecondary damned). During the right time we thought it was actually funny. He didn't just draw the six containers with stick-figures in 'em and the poorly graphed word bubbles like most young ones; he actually found out the proper structure to publish a book script that is comic. He kept trying to make us read them but – I mean – we didn't know how. Plus, we were busy. You understand, with school?

Anyway, Derek had this long bastard of a comic book script freshly printed from the school library – an adaptation of some classic horror story by Poe or Lovecraft, I think – and he ran up to Lloyd and me in the cafeteria all smiling, waving it us to read it at us, begging. And, remember, this ended up being the afternoon that is same got our abysmal test ratings back.

Now, despite our understandably mood that is pissy both Lloyd and I also resisted the urge to tear Derek's head off. Lloyd stated feebly,

"Sure, Derek. Give it here. I'll read it tonight."

Derek almost leapt down the table bench, he had been so excited. He thanked us then was off to God understands where.

I turned my mind and glowered at Lloyd.

"Are you serious?" He was expected by me. "You realize we now have presentation for Chemistry to finish tonight, right?"

Lloyd blew out the relative side of his mouth.

"I'm maybe not gonna read it, dude," he said, his eyes cast woefully down regarding the crumb and grease tabletop that is laden. "I'm just pranking him," he concluded, quarter-heartedly.

I sat here and stared at it for a seconds which are few. Then, another scheme that is mendacious spinning in my own mind.

I knew that my Uncle Eric had been coming over for supper that weekend. I told Lloyd that he had read his script and loved it that we would both inform Derek that my uncle worked for Marvel Comics and. And it and giving Derek a job writing for Stan Lee that he was interested in publishing. I'd invite Derek over to consult with him to discuss this "job prospect" at greater length. The one thing that is funny, my Uncle Eric was a belligerent drunk who'd mostly been unemployed between his time as a trucker and his time as a garbageman. But never – it probably does not need to be said– did he work with Marvel ever Comics.

Lloyd and I both giggled and grinned like wicked young ones. It had been perfect. This way, we wouldn't have to be drilled by Derek's questions in what was our part that is favourite would be too preoccupied by the idea of having his work really posted. Working for Marvel Comics for God's sake! An early Christmas present for our naïve friend that is young.

...I guess it is possible to probably determine just what happened next. I'll take to to spare you the facts being cringe-worthy.

The morning that is next Lloyd and we told Derek about my uncle and fed him our line. Derek beamed like I'd never seen before and bought it hook-line-and-sinker. Of course. That, he arrived over for dinner, all excited sunday. Of course. My Uncle Eric was two-sheets to your wind, six gin-and-tonics deep as well as on his seventh that night. Of course. So when Derek approached him, asking about his script and what it's like to work for Marvel, my Uncle Eric harshly barked what into the hell he had been blathering about. Needless to say.

I promised Lloyd I would give him most of the details on Monday. But Derek that is seeing over and defeated, like some withered daffodil – I just, had to look away. I did laugh that is n't. Didn't chuckle. Didn't even smirk. All i possibly could away do was look, that pit in my stomach looking at rock.

On, in front of the school entrance, about thirty minutes before first bell and thirty degrees below zero, Derek stormed right up to me monday. Indifferent, seeing this coming and finding no despair, surprise or pleasure I stood where I became and allow him hammer me personally in it.

Instead, there were no threats, no curses, no accusations. Only one question: did I lie about Christie Blackwell too?

Despite being exhausted through the endless stream of assignments and night's that is last guilt, I somehow managed the strength to slowly shake my head and mutter no. One prank that is last Derek.

With that, Derek said absolutely nothing. And simply stepped away.

At that minute, standing there alone with sticky icicles running down my lip that is top from nose to my scarf, we thought we would definitely provide.

The day that is next we advised Lloyd we give Derek some distance at lunch hour. I suspected we were personae non grata.

But, to my shock, Derek came over to our table. Stone-faced, without a expressed word he sat down and ate. Lloyd and I glanced over at him then at each and every other. The three of us just chewed and sat in silence.

Then, after completing his serving of oily cafeteria French fries, he told us one of his typically great, terrifying stories. His last.

"You guys ever hear about Melvin Sinclair?" he began, cryptically.

Fake-sounding name. Still, a pretty begin that is good.

Lloyd and I both shook our minds, wordlessly.

"He was a student at our college. Means right back, when the nuns ran it."

I later learned this right part of his story was true. Our high school – Pendleton College – was once run by the nunnery that is local but this was when it was nevertheless a residential school, with only bad, shipped-in Native kids as its student body.

"He's really the person i will write my comic-script that is next on. I understand you two won't read it, but I believe you ought to anyway learn about him.

"Sinclair was a kid that is funny. A little stupid, you know? Believed anything his pals told him."

This, needless to say, instantly rang a bell for both of us. Lloyd and I looked at each other knowingly. Nevertheless, we had been addicted. At the least, We was.

"He was also very poor with a father that is sick home who couldn't work. So, a complete great deal of his buddies might make him do things with the promise of money.

"So, one night, around this time of year – prior to Christmas, all those years ago, Sinclair and his buddies went out onto Saul Laskin Lake. It was frozen solid then, similar to it is at this time. Sinclair got dared by his buddies to walk out onto the lake – see it to the other side if he could make.

"Now, Sinclair was afraid. Terrified, you know? Saul Laskin is two soccer fields long and three areas wide. Sure, he knew it absolutely was frozen solid for 3 months straight and a jackhammer will make a dent n't an inch deep in it. But still, he was unsure. He never wandered across ice in the exact middle of winter prior to. Never even put a pair on of skates.

"To his buddies, he shook his head, no. He didn't care him a chicken if it made. He wasn't going nowadays, risking falling through.

"So, his friends made a decision to sweeten the deal. They told him so it to the other side, they'd meet him here, after walking across the shoreline, and pay him three-hundred dollars if he made.

"Now, their buddies didn't have three-hundred dollars, but they did have a wad that is thick of two-dollar bills. Therefore, they slipped one into Sinclair 's hand, as proof there clearly was more where that'd come from. They both figured it will be worth it to see Sinclair fall through the ice or wet himself from fear.

"Again, Sinclair wasn't too bright. He had been also very poor, and their household was method behind regarding the bill that is electric which had been bad since this was one of the worst winters in Canadian history. Never to mention, Christmas was right just about to happen. So, he took the two dollars as proof they had two-hundred-and-ninety-eight more making his way over the ice.

"The two of his friends giggled behind their mittens which are frozen-snot-covered egging him on, telling him he was doing great. Sinclair did clue that is n't though. He just kept going, waddling and swaying from side to side like a rope that is tight, terrified the rhino-hide-thick ice would give.

"Now, his two buddies did want Sinclair to n't get harmed. Not seriously anyway. At worst, they had been waiting until their bellies were sore for him to slip and fall on his ass, so they really could laugh at him.

"So, Sinclair got sixty foot across the ice when his buddies at the shore heard a crunch that is sudden. A sharp, unmistakable sound. The ice had cracked. Saul Laskin ended up being giving under Sinclair 's weight. Evidently, the lake wasn't so titanium at the center.

"Feeling a rapid rush of panic and just a little of guilt, both of them started hollering towards the top of their lung area for Sinclair to get the ice off. To turn straight back. Sinclair didn't turn around though. He didn't also stop walking. He had been determined to make it to one other side. To make that three hundred dollars. Cracks in the ice be damned, their house required heat!

"His pals on the coast viewed in horror when Sinclair took four more steps before plummeting through the ice in the 5th. Unable to think, being kids which are stupid they freaked and ran away. It took them 10 minutes they had a need to go get help before they realized.

"A couple of the nuns and something associated with farmers from city came out onto the ice. They made a horrific discovery when they got to the break where Sinclair had fallen in. On the other hand of the hole, was a collection of freshly frozen footprints. Like images within the snow but upside down and in out. They had been raised and glistening, like a trail of swollen scar-tissue. And they headed to the other side – to the final end of Saul Laskin Lake.

The five of these went to another side of the pond, coming to the extremely end, to get that the steps ended at an extra gaping hole into the ice"On the shoreline.

"Sinclair 's body was never discovered. But the medical practioners were particular it needs been impossible for him to have walked that length of the ice without succumbing to hypothermia.

"Ever since that night, in the anniversary of Melvin Sinclair 's arctic plunge, they say he comes back, still drenched and half-frozen rigid, looking for the three-hundred dollars promised him. And taking any heart that is regrettable dares wander across the ice, mistaking them for his two pals who had played that cruel joke on him, so very sometime ago."

Lloyd and I stared back at Derek speechless, our mouths agape.

The silence had been interrupted when two loud, chortling sophomores bumped into Derek from behind, making their means past him.

"This has to be bull," Lloyd insisted, rearing straight back from the dining table.

"Where'd you get this?" I asked, my eyes having never left face that is derek's.

"I said," he said. "It's the basis of my next script that is comic which you won't read. There are somethings out there that can't be understood. But they can be found by you out if you just suspend your disbelief."

I looked hard at him. He smirked.

"I heard it from one of this teachers and from one of the upper-classman year that is final" he confessed. "Both of them told the tale exactly as i recently did."

I was then fairly specific just what Derek had been planning to say next. And I also was appropriate.

"The anniversary of Melvin Sinclair 's disappearance is tonight," he whispered, as though we were sharing secrets which are state-level. "I say we get to Saul Laskin after dark and check it out."

Lloyd blew out his mouth, his lips making that 'pffft' sound.

"Yeah, all right," I said hastily. Very nearly automatically.

"What?" Lloyd blurted.

"I'll go," I proceeded. "Hell, let's all get."

"Great!" said Derek, over Lloyd's grumbled protest. "Meet you both at the shoreline near Tenth and Mockingbird. Be here at ten, sharp."

With that, Derek stood from their seat, carrying his meal tray towards the metal rack and exiting the caf.

"Dude," Lloyd spun on me personally. "What gives?"

"Look, man," I offered Lloyd, weakly. "We did something is actually lousy Derek. I think the smallest amount of we can do so invest one late night with him on this little whim."

"That's crap!" snapped Lloyd. "This is your means of playing another prank on him."

We shook my head vigorously, vexed by their charge. "No way!"

"Yeah? Well, maybe this is way that is derek's of us back. Playing a prank on us. You ever think about that?"

"I doubt it. Derek's nothing like that."

Lloyd just shook their mind, obviously pissed.

We didn't say such a thing after that. But the two of us knew, we had been planning to Saul Laskin Lake that to meet up with Derek evening.

Its remembered by me was ten below zero. Felt like minus twenty with the wind and even worse that near to the ice. The stars had been probably out, and fully visible, but we don't' remember seeing them. We could barely see exactly what was in front of me from my face two-thirds which are being behind my scarph and tuque.

We met Lloyd on the real method there, about ten yards from the shoreline on Mockingbird, and he was likewise dressed like a winter mummy. We saw a figure standing upright, unfazed by the cutting gale as we got closer. It was Derek. He had been in their snow-pants and a parka but ended up being something that is n't putting on cover his head. Just a pair of earmuffs. Bizarrely, he seemed completely comfortable nowadays, his flushed red cheeks the point that is only exactly how cold he was.

"Well, here we are,us, cryptically" he greeted. A just as cryptic laugh on his chapped, purple lips.

"What are we doing out here?" Lloyd growled, rubbing their thickly fingers that are gloved and bouncing in one base to the other. "It's freezing!"

"We're here to see if Melvin Sinclair 's ghost turns up," I told him.

The look I had been distributed by him could have thawed Saul Laskin Lake.

"I never said it absolutely was a ghost," said Derek, right above the wind.

Us stared at our guide into the other globe.

"Then just what is it?" I asked.

"A zombie?" Lloyd mocked.

Feigning lack of knowledge, Derek just shrugged.

The three of us just stood there, in the center of December in Canada, observing the pond that is frozen three wallflowers around a dancefloor (an analogy that's not much of a stretch for us).

Predictably, Derek broke the silence.

"How he asked about we play some Truth or Dare. We viewed and saw that smile that is cryptic their now bluish lips.

"How about we play some Go-Home-And-Sleep-In-A-House-With-Central-Heating?" Lloyd barked.

Me personally, we couldn't help myself.

"Sure," I said. "Let's play some Truth or Dare."

"You first," Derek pounced.

Ordinarily, we could have bickered back and forth with Derek to try to get him to get first, but my conscience that is recently-grown forced to accept this problem.

"Okay," I said. I then looked out onto the ice, anticipating what the dare can be and lacking any from it. "Truth."

For the full time that is first evening, Derek's strange smirk disappeared.

"All right," he said, their face and voice now extremely severe. "Yesterday morning," my mind then straight away raced compared to that moment, regretting my choice for Truth, "when I asked you about Christie Blackwell,"

"Okay, okay, never ever mind!" I shouted before he may even get the question out over him. "I changed my mind. Dare. Offer me personally a dare. What? I am desired by you to definitely walk across the lake? Is the fact that it?"

Without speaking, Derek nodded their head, that cryptic grin reappearing that is little.

I then seemed back at the pond that is frozen. Derek hadn't lied whenever he said that it ended up being two football fields long. In reality, it had been much longer. 273.5 yards to be precise. The other side swallowed up by night and fog from where we were standing, I could see only half of the ice.

"Okay, here's a deal," we said, attempting to negotiate my way out of it. "I'll go so far as whenever that fog starts. That's just me. before you two won't be able to see"

"No deal," said Derek, his eyes colder than Saul Laskin. "You get all of the way across, or that you're scared to go out there. until you see Melvin Sinclair, or you admit you believed my story enough"

“What?”

“Or choose Truth.”

“I'm not scared of that boogeyman crap!” I exclaimed.

“Then have you thought to go most of the way?” said Derek. “You know that lake is perfectly safe for skating. It's been frozen solid since. october”

“Because it is stupid, that's why.”

“Or because you're Melvin that is afraid Sinclair get you.”

“No, I'm not.”

“Fine. Then choose Truth. Answer my question.”

Astonished, I shot him a look that is incredulous.

"Man, screw you!" I cried. "You're the one who's so stupid you think that story that is stupid. You probably did hear it from an upper-classman 12 months that is final. They knew you'd be gullible enough to buy it."

I turned to the pond that is frozen my eyes melting the ice.

"I'm going to go in terms of that fog begins. From there, I'll manage to see over to one other side. I'll additionally be appropriate within the middle therefore it will prove a couple of things: One, that no one could fall through the ice when it's this cold out, and two, that there clearly wasn't some creature that is supernatural around through the night. I'll prove to you there's no such thing."

Derek seemed back at me. That smile that is strange again from his lips and never came back.

"I'm not gullible," he insisted in a voice that is low. "The story is true."

"Ah, up yours," I stated, walking to the edge of the shoreline and shuffling gingerly onto the ice. "Come on, Lloyd. Let's go."

"Me?" I heard from behind.

"Come on, you wimp. Let's show this moron how full and stupid of it he's."

The two of us waddled onto Saul Laskin. We inched our method closer and closer to the middle that is foggy the dense air never seeming to thin out and recede like it ordinarily would. Truthfully, I could barely see an inch in-front of me; the whipping, cool atmosphere caused me to tear up and turned my tears to icicles on my lashes. But I happened to be too angry to care. In my mind, I told myself I just wanted to prove to Derek exactly what an idiot he had been. In fact, I simply desired anyway to avoid telling him the reality about Christie Blackwell.

We were well past the center-point when I finally decided to get rid of. Lloyd was a bit ahead of me. We seemed around. The fog was so dense. Even worse, I'd to rapidly blink my eyes to break up the frozen moisture that accumulated on my lashes.

We roughly cleared my gloved thumb to my eyesight. And then it was seen by me personally. A figure that is hunched just obscured by the fog, hobbling slowly toward Lloyd. Lloyd must-have been having exactly the same difficulty I became, though it had been practically right in his line of sight because he made no effort to operate or talk to the figure, even.

In the beginning, it was thought by me was Derek. Thought he had somehow caught up and was wanting to scare us. But I Became incorrect. I was very, very wrong.

I attempted to warn Lloyd. To shout out. To ask who ended up being there. But I couldn't. The words were trapped in my neck. I became since petrified as the ice I stood upon. I stared, seeing the figure that 's almost naked into focus. It ended up being a man – or...what was once a man. The skin was pale, translucent, most of the blue and veins that are purple. The hair was– that is blonde and slicked back, like your head had just been submerged in water. It seemed like a cadaver that had escaped from the populous city morgue. Its eyes that are brightly-colored a pair of round broken mirrors, and never once did I see them near. Perhaps not even blink.

Then, it speak i... I heard!

"I did it..." it muttered, hoarsely, the sound such as the ruffling of crumpled paper. "I did it...where is she?"

The creature had been foot that are mere Lloyd, but he'd switched their back to it like it wasn't there. He then lifted their mind, one eye that is red, and asked, "Jimmy? Did you say–"

Before he could complete, the walking cadaver shot a long, bony supply, grasping its claw-like fingers to his shoulder.

Lloyd looked around and shrieked.

"Where is she?" the thing muttered huskily. "Where's my infant?"

Certainly terrified, Lloyd tried to sprint away, just to slide and fall on the ice. The cadaver's that is walking remained unbroken, causing Lloyd's cold weather coat to rip. The fact pinned him onto the ice, its grasping claws Lloyd that is shaking by lapels.

"You said it, you'd tell me personally where she was!" it hissed into Lloyd's face if we did. I viewed, nevertheless petrified, only able to imagine the look of confusion and terror on Lloyd's face that is bundled-up.

"Where is she!" the creature screamed. "Where is she? You promised. You promised*!" * Its sound cracked on the syllable that is last.

It then started throwing Lloyd's torso up and down, until the back of their head hit the ice with a thud that is shuddering. We cringed. It absolutely was just like the sound of a bowling ball being dropped straight to the tiled, wooden floor. The thing then mounted him, clawing and punching at their lifeless form in a frenzy that is hungry. With its cracked, blackened teeth bared, the canines resembled a set of fangs.

We wanted to run. I wished to help – to fight that simple thing off of my pal. But I swear, I – I couldn't.

By the time that thing had stopped, I could see freshly fallen droplets which are red steaming in the ice around Lloyd's head. We knew then that he was gone.

What took place next, I can't explain. The creature laid straight down on Lloyd's supine body, putting its pale, grotesquely scabbed mind on his chest, as though listening for a heartbeat. When I knew that the fog was thickening. There had been entire plumes of smoke wafting up from the ice beneath their figures. I realized when they began to sink, that the ice was melting.

The creature sunk down underneath the ice, pulling my friend's carcass along side it. Once they had slipped out of sight, we heard the sound that is worst you can perhaps imagine. The noise of the ice cracking. I looked over my feet and saw a gash that is deeply shaped like a lightning bolt, tearing a path through the ice beneath my foot and between my feet. Several mini fractures splintered off, producing a spider-web of icy shards.

My senses coming back to me, we went, stumbling and falling, right back to the shoreline. I don't know how steps that are many created before I slid and fell through – and was completely submerged in Saul Laskin.

I don't remember just how cool it was – though it was freezing beyond imagination. I simply remember the disgusting feeling of my clothes soaking into the water beside my skin– and the panic that is sheer inside my skull.

Remember how we ended up being fat and short? Well, I also didn't have a clue how exactly to swim. I just floated there, beneath the water, not seeing something which is damned my brain a riot of horrible scenarios and pictures.

At me personally and pull as you would expect, I flailed in desperate mortal fear when we felt a hand grab. Thankfully, the tactile hand had been pulling me personally upward, to safety. And it belonged to Derek.

"Jimmy," Derek panted, up onto the surface after he'd dragged me personally. "It's – it's okay,as he too was drenched from head to toe" he struggled to state. "Here's my – my coat…p-put it on."

He then laid his parka that is open over body. Luckily, it absolutely was taken by him off before scuba diving in to save me. I'm sure now if it wasn't for his thinking that is quick have died that night.

"L-listen – listen to me," he stammered on. Their lips were switching a deep blue, as was his face. "My phone is in just one of the coat pockets, call 9-1-1."

"W-what?" I stated, not understanding why he didn't do it himself.

"Just do it," he said, then turned and began walking into the direction of that creature.

"Wait!"

"I'm – I'm going to g-g-go get L-l-l-loyd!" he blurted down. Now, this is where I'd like to inform you that I forced Derek to stay beside me. Him the reality about Christie Blackwell that I told. With Lloyd and my Uncle Eric that I apologized for the cruel laugh we had played on him. And for always taking him and his friendship for granted. But that didn't happen. Shivering from the cold and my fear that is own just watched as he marched away, vanishing to the fog.

I took down his phone from the pocket that is right dialed 9-1-1. I recall hearing the telephone ring, the sound that is monotonous in my skull. We don't remember anyone answering.

Finished . that is final remember is the sense of my body growing warm. All the fear and discomfort evaporating with the fog. Then, there was blackness. Blackness conserve for a horoscope of horrible images playing on a loop in my head.

I woke up into the emergency room.

I was told that the paramedics and fire department were called out. That they'd scanned the ice but never found Derek or Lloyd. I happened to be told that We was fortunate to be alive. Even luckier that i did son't have frostbite and would therefore not have to lose any appendages.

Ultimately, they got around to asking me why we had been on the market and exactly what happened. They certainly were told by me everything. Every detail that is last. Of program, they all looked I happened to be crazy at me like. Some of them also thought me undergo a CAT scan that I might have gone into shock and asked my parents to have. I never ever did though.

Within my time within the hospital, three thoughts kept spinning around my brain. One, just how grateful I became to Derek Zimmer for saving my life. Two, how surprised I was that their story was actually true. And three, why that creature kept requesting its child, instead of for cash, like in Derek's story. I learned later that the tale Derek had told us that afternoon was one of the main legends Saul that is concerning Laskin and that night. Some were about a man whose daughter was in fact kidnapped by a gang of thieves; that the man had been thrown in to the lake, their legs encased in concrete, after he'd paid their ransom. Some had been of a lady that is mentally disturbed had drowned her baby, thinking it was possessed by the devil. And at the very least half dozen more I can't here stomach reciting.

Perhaps the minute that is worst after that night was when I got a check out from Missus Calhoun, the principal at Pendleton College.

She was in her early seventies, stout, with a tight, silver bob cut
and moobs of owlish spectacles on her round, little nose. She sat
down at my bedside, wearing her shapeless, riotously patterned
muumuu, and asked me exactly what had happened at Saul Laskin.
She was told by me personally. The tale that is exact same had told
everyone since waking up in the er. She simply stared at me,
expressionless, before giving out a sharp sigh through her small
nostrils when I was done.

"This is what I think occurred, James," she began, a disdain that is
subtle her voice. "I think you dared Lloyd Apanowicz and Derek to
there go out on the ice. We all know how you tortured and tricked
that bad boy since primary school.

"I think whenever the ice cracked, and your friends fell in, you
panicked and arrived up with this lie that is ludicrous cover your
tracks, because you think we're all as gullible as poor Derek
Zimmer. Us are that dumb because you think you're that smart
additionally the rest of. I think you're a cruel, immature,
sociopathic boy that is little wind up becoming a cheat and a fraud
and invest his adult life in and out of prison."

From my sleep, we stared back at her wide-eyed. It absolutely was
so surreal. An adult – a trained teacher– speaking in my
experience in a way.

"And I don't care who you tell this to," she hissed. Year"Because I'm retiring by the end of this college. And like you once again, it'll be too quickly. if we never see another sadistic child"

I had been rescued, had nearly succumbed to hypothermia myself, she grunted and said, "I don't understand once I raised just how. You seem all right in my experience. After all, you didn't even get frostbite available to you, did you? And you're the only person of those men whom survived."

She then shook her head that is grey me, making a tsk-tsk-tsk noise with her tongue.

"In and out of jail," she repeated to herself, before increasing from her seat and leaving me on personal.

Today, I'm thrilled to tell you her prognosis was false. I have actuallyn't been in prison at any moment in my life and the i've that is worst ever gotten is a speeding ticket. That being said, shame has followed me around now ever since that night.

We never ever told Derek i will be eternally sorry that I had lied about Christie Blackwell, as well as for that. Across the frozen pond as I am for making Lloyd come with me. I had also doubted Derek about his story regarding the spirit that haunts Saul Laskin annually on a December evening, just a weeks being few of Christmas. For that too, my apologies.

I don't know what compelled me to play numerous tricks on him, besides my overly logical, and nature that is cynical. But ever since that, I'm not so quick to dismiss something – even if it can seem fantastic night. Or even impossible.

THE ELF ON THE SHELF IS A FICTIONAL CHARACTER

Growing up, or at least since the thousands that are mid-two the house constantly had an Elf on the Shelf during the Christmas period. In the event that you don't know, Elves in the Shelf are these elf that is small which are likely to be scouts for Santa Claus. We named mine Humble. I do believe I was wanting to name him Humboldt but got the words confused, I wanted to mention him Humboldt in the first place though i've long forgotten why. Anyway, starting every Thanksgiving, my parents would stick Humble somewhere he could practice their espionage that is domestic at night he would head straight back to the North Pole to snitch on me personally to Santa. He constantly travelled back before dawn, always hiding someplace new, and each morning was like a Easter that is miniature egg to find him.

Of program, it had been my moms and dads who moved the thing that is damn night. We guess i've some feelings that are blended the tradition. On the one hand, it had been fun and magical, but in the other, it is a pretty expansion that is aggressive the practice of using Santa to help keep your children in line. I've also heard people say it normalizes government and surveillance that is corporate however in age Alexa and Google, that's a bit of a moot point.

But I think the matter that is weirdest about the Elf on the Shelf is how I was never allowed to touch the doll. I could communicate with him, tell him the things I wanted Santa to bring me for Christmas and all that, but touching him may empty him of his miracle and keep him from time for the North Pole where he belonged. Here's the line that is actual the storybook that accompany the doll.

"There's only one rule so i am going to come back and be here tomorrow: Please do not touch me personally you need to follow. My miracle may go, and Santa won't hear all I've seen or I understand."

Demonstrably, the taboo against touching the doll makes it harder for a kid to conceive around– or worse, testing that theory – which to me really feels extremely manipulative that it's actually their moms and dads moving it. That would be after I stopped believing in Santa because I never actually moved Humble, even years. I have two younger siblings, so I guess We could rationalize it as not touching him for their sake, but component that is… of just could not overcome the taboo about maybe not touching the doll that my mother had instilled in me personally.

I'm eighteen now as well as in college, living in a condo that is off-campus. We went home for Thanksgiving, of program, and sure enough, Humble was there on the mantlepiece. My sister Jenna loves the creeper that is little full-heartedly believing he's magic and works for Santa Claus. We felt a little guilty, her purchasing the whole story hook, line, and sinker, but decided it absolutely was none of my company.

I had been supposed to head back again to my apartment, my mother asked me because covertly as she could if I knew where Humble was whenever I got up Sunday morning, the afternoon. He was missing, and no one in my household did actually know where he went or will be prone to play such a cruel trick on our member that is youngest. Whenever he couldn't be found, my mom took Jenna aside and tried to explain that Humble must have been storm stayed at Santa's Workshop. To everyone's surprise, Jenna was delighted during the news. She said that she stressed about me personally living away from home, and asked if he could spend time at my apartment to make sure I became safe, and that's where he must be that she told Humble.

My mother eagerly went along with this, as I surely got to my apartment to verify that Humble ended up being safe and sound, *wink wink* since it gave her time to locate a replacement doll, and explained to call as quickly. We promised to call the second I got in, and after saying my farewells, We embarked on the drive that is hours-long to my apartment.

I managed to reunite before dark, which of course comes obscenely early this time of year, and I caught a glimpse of something bright red standing out against the off-white of my kitchenette when I awkwardly tried to make my way through the entranceway along with my travel bags at once.

It was Humble, sitting atop his legs to my Keurig crossed and his hands in their lap. It ended up being known by me was Humble because my mother had placed a bell from a Lindt chocolate bunny around his waist like a belt and stuck a miniature candy cane in it.

The situation that is normally upsetting of breaking into my apartment was tempered by the actual fact that it had obviously been a member of my family, but who, and why?

As opposed to calling them I took an image and texted it to my mom using the message 'Did you do this?' like I promised,.

Moments later the discussion that is following:

'Sweetie, y would u steal Humble? U understand how ur that is much loves him'.

'Mom, I swear, I didn't steal him. I just discovered him here once I got home. Because we know we locked up before I left. in the event that you didn't try this, check always to help make certain you still have my spare key,'

'K, we just examined. It's right where it will b. I asked ur father, in which he doesn't know any such thing either. He's looking over the security camera footage to make sure we weren't broken directly into. Sweetie, we swear we didn't do this. Maybe u should come back home or stay in a hotel until we figure this out.'

A hidden intruder, one thing missing or damaged, and found nothing at this point I've searched my entire apartment for any sign of forced entry. The sole thing out of place is Humble, and it makes no sense that is goddamn.

Probably the most likely explanation was that someone within my family was messing i really couldn't consider anybody who would do this to me and Jenna, let alone have been able to have taken Humble, drive to my apartment, stick it, and then drive back undetected with me, but. The only real other explanation that is logical that I had an extremely stealthy, very skilled stalker who'd chosen an oddly specific option to mess with me.

Of course, there was a clear description that is irrational where Humble came from, but we turn off that line of idea immediately. It's just a doll that is damn.

I actually didn't want to operate a vehicle anymore and decided I couldn't miss course the day that is next waste money on a resort, therefore I asked my boyfriend to invest the evening, who was more than happy to oblige. That still left the presssing dilemma of how to handle it with Humble. Demonstrably, I should've just mailed him home, but that would've required that he is moved by me.

That had to be why it ended up being done by them. They knew I happened to be nevertheless afraid to touch Humble and these people were teasing me. Which had become it. However it was carried out by them, that had to be it.

This had been good though, I thought. My unwillingness to touch Humble was childish, and I was all grown-up now. I needed to move past it. The doll was sitting there on my coffee maker. All I had to do was grab him, place him in a box, and deliver him away. My little sister gets her doll back, and I become just a bit that is small mature. There was no reason that is rational to do it.

I truthfully can't inform you how long I just stood here, staring at Humble, trying to muster the courage up to pick him up. It was absurd, but i recently couldn't do it. My mother had ingrained that taboo into me too damn well, and Humble that is pressing would like crushing a fairy.

"Hey, Humble," we started mumbling. "I understand my sibling asked one to keep an eye I know you're just trying to make her happy, but you're supposed to be watching her to report back again to Santa, remember on me, and? You are known by me accustomed view me, but I'm grown-up now. I don't even get presents from Santa anymore. You don't need to watch me, and I'd hate for your report on Jenna to be inaccurate because you're here and never there. So please, her know I'm doing fine. when you report back into the North Pole today, get back to Jenna and let" The cupboard had been opened by me and pulled out a pack of blueberry turnovers, placing one beside Humble. "That's for Santa. I understand it's probably maybe not his kind that is favorite of, but it's all I have right now. Merry Christmas, Humble."

I don't understand why those ideas were said by me personally. I don't know why he was given by me the cookie. I didn't actually believe he was one of Santa's Elves. At least, I don't think used to do.

My boyfriend Sean arrived soon after that. He didn't mention it if he noticed Humble. He's a pretty typical guy that is college-age so was eager to get to our bed room activities, and I happened to be hopeful for anything to have my brain off of Humble, so we got straight to it. I decided that for me if I still couldn't find the will to box up Humble each morning, I'd simply asked Sean to complete it.

I woke up the next morning in a considerably better mood, courtesy of this night's afterglow that is previous. Sean had been nevertheless sound asleep that I would personally have to go him to make my coffee beside me personally, per usual, after which we

remembered Humble, and. I thought about waking Sean up myself
i was being absurd and to just get it done myself for it, but told.

However when we opened my bedroom home and looked into my
kitchenette, Humble was gone, and so was the cookie.

My first thought ended up being that Sean must have relocated
him at some point, nevertheless the time that is only ever got out
of bed was to use the washroom, which was next to the bedroom
and didn't connect to the living area. He'd proven himself time and
time once again to be completely not capable of escaping . of sleep
without waking me up, so there was no genuine way he went here
while I happened to be resting. Also he never would have cleaned
up the cookie if he had. He might have eaten it, however might
have gone for many left the package out (I know I'm not making
him seem great here, but he's mostly a drinking/bang buddy and
I'm not planning on us being a long-term thing).

I straight away started looking for Humble, trying to find where
within my apartment that is tiny he could have gone, whenever I
heard a notification from my phone, particularly the main one I
had set for texts from my sibling. I sudden dread swept over me
personally, a fear of a thing that needs to have been impossible
somehow becoming truly the only description that is conceivable.

I picked up my phone, swiped it open, and once I clicked on
messages, I saw a photo of Humble sitting on my sister's bed, with
the writing that is accompanying

'Humble's straight back! I am wanted by him to inform you that Santa states thanks for the blueberry cookie. Chocolate chip's his favorite, but it absolutely was still yummy!'

I became in shock, after that. I did son't understand what to think. How could someone have stolen the doll, brought it here, snuck it out again, and then brought it house without leaving any sort of evidence? And why? I acquired another text from my Mom later, whom seemed content to compose the whole thing off she ever made us believe about the doll as me and my sibling playing a trick on her behalf as payback for everything. I insisted we weren't, but soon provided up. I couldn't blame my Mom for thinking that. It's what i might have thought if I was in her position. I wish I had been in her position, instead of trying to figure down if I became being stalked, haunted by a doll that is possessed or simply going insane.

We was able to rule out the option that is first quickly. I set up my phone to record the living space throughout the night. No one came into the front door, and there was clearlyn't the sound that is slightest of anybody coming in through any windows. And yet, come morning, there was Humble, cozied up in the camera's spot that is blind. There ended up being not a way anyone could there have put him. I still couldn't move him though, and I was through talking to him. This time Sean did enquire about the doll, but all he had been told by me was "It's my sister's, don't touch it", and he shrugged it down.

We set up my phone to record Humble that, but it automatically restarted for updates and Humble escaped back again to my sister unseen evening. It's been going on like this for weeks now, Humble going back and forth between me and my sister. I've had Sean over every evening, but I didn't make sure he understands why however, exactly that I required the dopamine boost, and that I desired because much time together as feasible ahead of the Christmas Break split us up that I was stressed with exams and also the holidays and. He didn't complain.

I don't know the things I thought I was being protected by him from. Humble was just a doll, and he had never shown any indications me any damage which he meant. He had been just a scout elf doing his job. It's– that is funny the phenomenon that has been causing me a great deal terror was delighting my sibling, and might have pleased me once I was younger. To Jenna, a toy moving forward its own was all right part of the Holiday magic. To me, it absolutely was an omen that the international globe did not operate just how I thought it did, and forced me to concern my really sanity.

Yesterday, Friday the 20th, ended up being the day that is last of. Humble was with my sis, and my boyfriend caught an overnight Greyhound to their family members, that I became on my own so it was 1st evening in almost three weeks. My plan was to operate a vehicle back to my family on since I didn't want to drive that far at night saturday. This could, of course, mean I'd be kept alone with Humble when he returned in the early morning, that I coped with through my normal weekly ritual of exorbitant drinking that is underage.

I woke up today like I do most Saturdays; with a mild to moderate hangover and just a vague recollection for the night that is previous. We reached over to try to nudge my boyfriend to get me some coffee, only to keep in mind he wasn't there. We groaned and forced myself out of sleep, stumbled out into the living area, and – just as I had expected I'm that is– greeted Humble.

Except that today, he's leaned up contrary to the door that is front. The apartment can't be left by me– not without moving him. We was trapped.

I completely broke straight down then, dropping down seriously to my knees and sobbing, demanding to understand why he was tormenting me like this. We hadn't done anything other than grow up.

That's when I understood that, as I thought since I have was crying and screaming at a doll, maybe I wasn't as grown-up. I had thought that taking on five figures in figuratively speaking, getting shitfaced at the very least once a week, and settling for a boyfriend that is practical all meant We was an adult, but I guess I had been wrong.

Humble had been supposed to get his power from the love of the young youngster who owned him, and which used to be me. I suppose that by never overcoming my reluctance to move him, We hardly ever really broke that bond, and he had been legitimately split between me and Jenna. That basically was it then, wasn't it? All I had to do was shove him apart. We could even just ask anyone to come over and whenever they arrived in Humble is pushed out just of the means, but even that felt wrong somehow. As harrowing as this experience that is entire been, there clearly was still some part of me that was enchanted by the magic of it all, a part of me that a lot of people lost a long time ago, and it was a part of that I still ended up beingn't ready to give up. And how about Jenna? My sweet little sibling who loves her elf doll and nevertheless wanted to share him that she'd know I'd be safe by myself beside me so. I really couldn't take away her experiencing Christmas that is actual Magic could I?

I took another photo of Humble and texted it to Jenna, explaining me personally inside and I also wouldn't be coming house until the next day that he had trapped. She comprehended entirely – she would never ever dare to move Humble either. Of program, a minutes which can be few I got a call from my Mom, and she ended up being livid. She thought I was just too hungover to get back, ranting exactly how this was going to throw the Holiday plans off and what an irresponsible drunk I ended up being switching into. Given that I'm presently coping with the incident that is whole dipping into a bottle of cherry schnapps I got as an early Christmas gift, I can't say she's wrong.

I'm still in my apartment now. Humble hasn't relocated, of program, and I can't force myself to move him. I'm maybe not mad at him. We don't think he's achieving this to hurt me. I believe he just seriously believes I'm still one of is own kids, and he's doing his job the very best he can. Today's been rough, but is supposed to be better tomorrow. He'll head back to my sister, I'm sure. Why wouldn't he? That's what he's been doing for the last three weeks. He'll be out of my way and I'll be able to leave and head back home. My mom will have calmed down and just be happy to have me personally home and everything will be perfect, though she'll probably attempt to talk me into doing January that is dry with. All that matters is beside me and my sister under the roof that is same Humble will stay placed until Christmas Eve, and then this nightmare before Christmas will all be over. Year at least, until next.

Maybe by then I'll be a bit more grown-up.

THE WHITE CHRISTMAS

Surviving in reduced Alabama, we rarely get snow. I spent nearly all of my life wishing for a Christmas that is white white Christmas that never came. We have only seen snow twice in my thirty-three years here. We always wished to share that with my two boys. We just knew that they'd love to relax and play in it. Now we find myself staring out my window at the mounds of this precipitation that is icy my home, regretting every wish I had ever designed for a snow-covered Christmas.

It, it really began in summer time whenever We think of. Our summers are constantly hot and very humid but that it had been more intolerable year. We steadily saw temperatures of well over a hundred degrees and everyone else I knew begged for relief. The heatwave lasted all the way until the before Halloween week. Then suddenly, a hurricane that is massive in the Gulf of Mexico. The weather forecaster for our news that is local frequently to it as a "Monster". Searching right back it will be thought by me was more of a demon. A demon that brought Hell than I had read about into the Bible along with it, but a much different one.

The storm passed, leaving devastation for miles around. It had affected every ongoing state in the southeast but Florida first and foremost. Help was delivered from various energy organizations, government aid agencies, and citizens being even regular help utilizing the relief. And when I state various, I mean out of every constant state inside our area. It was amazing to start to see the effort put forth to aid the social individuals who had lost everything. I am sure a complete large amount of us thought that was the worst it could get. I wish that have been true, but that was if the rainfall started.

As November came, we felt the droplets that are first our small town. It was an occurrence that is odd however odd sufficient to boost any eyebrows. I suggest, how bad could a few days of rain be, right? The issue came when days turned into months and low areas that are lying inundated. Houses in towns nearby were washed away in a matter of hours when the levees broke. My spouse Susan constantly thanked God our home was nestled on a elevation that is high trees. I discovered myself thinking the thing that is same God had nothing in connection with what took place, no God I could ever have confidence in any way.

The of Thanksgiving the rain finally subsided and I am certain was something everyone else would say they were thankful for week. The situation was, what remained ended up being the cool. That, it was in itself, was perhaps not strange nevertheless the severity of. We saw temperatures close to freezing for the week that is following that was something we rarely saw until belated January or early February. My son that is oldest, Jacob, started singing that silly song by Bing Crosby. My wife beamed at the thought of these snow that is seeing Christmas time. The kid that is foolish me felt the same.

"The guys will finally get to see snow, Paul!" Susan squealed.

"I know, we can't wait to see Tommy waddling inside it!" We responded.

Those words ring in my own head even now. I have to fight back tears once I consider exactly how stupid I had been. We were so preoccupied with setting up decorations and presents that are buying we had been oblivious to what ended up being taking place around us. The snowfall actually started falling the week that is to begin. It had been up several ins inside the day that is first. It was amazing to see at first but when it kept coming, some social people became concerned. It snows, you probably would not understand if you've got never been in the south when. You see, we are perhaps not prepared for that kind or form of weather. Everything shuts down, people remain house and rarely head out driving. It is famous by me personally sounds ridiculous to other people, but that is really what happens.

It just kept coming. My wife and I had allow the boys perform in the fresh powder originally nevertheless when it had gotten so saturated in it freely, we decided it was best to have them indoors that we could scarcely walk. Hardware stores had started getting snowfall shovels to help paths that are clear a thing that you rarely found inside our town. I purchased among the last ones on the shelf, as people scrambled to manage the icy invader that is international. The problem seemed to be worse, as little flurries became near blizzards. My wife stayed glued to your climate and news broadcasts. It appeared the north states had almost been buried in the powder that is frigid. The President had actually given a state of emergency, urging individuals in the part that is northern evacuate south.

Which was once I finally began to be concerned. These individuals had been told to come south but our situation was hardly much better. The weatherman stopped trying to be accurate, their predictions of an final end towards the madness never came. The conditions continued to drop also it was not long them go from zero to negative digits before we saw. It absolutely was uncommon in my own state because of it become that cold and people had been getting afraid. Plumbing fixtures began to burst from frozen pipes and people were left without water until they could thaw. The world had become a freezer in a weeks that are few none of us were ready for this. My loved ones discovered themselves using our clothing that is thickest even inside. It felt like no matter how high the thermostat is defined by me personally, it had been perhaps not enough. We needs to have left then.

By Christmas, we had no power and utility organizations had stopped wanting to traverse the harsh conditions to repair lines that are downed. Neighborhood officials had abandoned emergency protocols to save your self themselves. We started hearing rumors of our next-door neighbors attempting to south head further into Florida. Susan suggested the same, but we reminded her associated with destruction still left from the hurricane. I was afraid we will be worse off without shelter. So, your decision was created by me to hunker down in our house. I cleared a path to the fireplace that had only been useful for set and decoration to the duty of having a fire going. In me attempting something like that when it had not been such a dire situation, my wife would have found amusement. We had never even seen someone utilize a fireplace, let light one alone.

After several attempts, we had been able to burn off what lumber that is little was readily available near our house. My family and I huddled around it as from the fate that waited outside if it had been going to save your self us. The whiteness had engulfed our home. The mounds had risen above the windows, breaking some of those. I had been forced to reinforce every one to help keep the cold out. We sealed every crack or crevice that may possibly allow the temperature out and attempted to remain together. My wife wrapped our kiddies in blankets and pulled them near. The males did not understand so we had been afraid to tell them how serious the situation was. The fear that rested on my wife's face had been enough to keep me personally from ruining what could possibly be our last Christmas.

We nevertheless attempted to own a dinner that is big despite our ability to effectively cook. I also discovered how to cook within a fireplace for the time that is first. It would have been an experiment that is interesting it had maybe not been essential for our survival at the time. We gave up in the idea of turkey or ham but we had always had a stock that is decent of food. It was a habit We had selected up from my grandparents. We frequently wondered how they were faring during all of this but I had my family that is immediate to about. Our world was plunged into an sea that is endless of. I even had nightmares of the stuff that Christmas Eve.

My kids normally woke me early on Christmas morning but when my eyes fluttered available I assumed it ended up being night that is still. The home was so dark that I could barely see my wife lying next to me. I gradually rose from my bed, still entirely nudged and clothed Susan awake. The house had become far colder we instantly headed for the fireplace than it should have been and. The fire had gone out at some point, so I ran for the entranceway that is back pulling on my boots. My aim was to gather more timber to get the fire going once more but as soon as the hinged home cracked open I had been pelted with a mixture of snow and ice. It stung my face and I also cursed during the hinged door while attempting to shut it again. Our home had been buried in the powder that is vicious we finally understood why no light permeated the windows. My view read nine-o'clock but it felt much earlier.

Susan stumbled in to the living space, asking what I became doing. She was told by me what time it absolutely was and confusion filled her eyes. She went for the window and was greeted with what we already knew. I actually do not remember ever seeing her quite therefore afraid and the feeling was mutual. I buried my emotions down though, once you understand I had to be strong for my household. I told her to go check in the young kids while I tried to get the fire going again. She disappeared down the hall and I also made my solution to the living area. The table and chairs had been passed down through my children for generations but it had been known by me will have to be sacrificed. I set to dismantling the chairs which are wood but had been stopped by the sound of my wife's scream.

I rushed through the hallway listening to the sound that is awful in my own ears. I could feel rips forming in my eyes but these were forced by me straight back as We rounded the corner. She was grasping the hinged door framework of our children's room. We had put them together in order that Jacob could help to keep an optical eye on Tommy. She could be seen by me body shaking as she stared into the space. Tears rolled over her cheeks as we looked to see inside. The window of these room had directed at the weight of our captor, despite my attempt at strengthening it. Snow had buried the men in the and that was when I noticed the flakes of white all over my wife's hands night. Susan had attempted to uncover them and I also could see the pale skin that is blue of faces, huddled together in Jacob's bed. It would have been a scene that is sweet it were not for their skin tone, something Susan would took a picture of but this was not that scene.

I pulled Susan away as I tried to hold back the feeling that is unwell my belly. I felt as on the floor at any time though i really could release what little Christmas supper I had in me personally. Soon her sobs subsided but when I looked she simply looked numb into her eyes. I'd never seen her this real way and I tried to break her from this trance she was in but she said nothing. Her eyes wouldn't normally turn my way even if I spoke. Something had broken inside Susan that and I do not blame her morning. I sat her next to your fireplace and wrapped her in a blanket while We returned to the dining room. The wood that is polished not want to burn off but I had been determined to provide us with warmth. So, I would not stop until we had fire.

I made it a point to ask Susan to stay by the fire while I returned to the boys room that is. I could perhaps not leave them that real way but when I reached the door i came across myself pausing simply outside. I felt the warm and salty specks across my cheeks before I even saw them. I slowly stepped inside and slid gloves over my arms. I completed clearing away the snow and noticed why they had not merely visited our room. The wood I'd utilized to seal the window off had struck my oldest first. It left a gash near his temple that could have knocked a man that is grown. I possibly could only imagine their body that is ten-year-old had lasted long after. Tommy had obviously woken after, his form that is tiny clung his big bro like a teddy bear. We internally cursed myself for not placing them to bed I knew it was far too late for that kind of thinking with us that night but. We removed their bodies and wrapped them in blankets before placing them in the guest room.

I took one look that is final their small bedroom, a place that had held therefore much joy previously. I imagined the pair of them playing and sometimes bickering. My lips tried to curl upward but they could not. My eyes drooped to a floor as I turned away and shut the home. I have not returned compared to that available space since and I also doubt I will. I just returned to the living room in hopes of reassuring Susan but when I got here the blanket was all that remained by the fire. A quick search of your home revealed that the rear door was opened and a tunnel had formed in the wall that is frigid one other part, leaving the floor inside covered in snow.

I tried to follow along with Susan's footsteps but fundamentally, they disappeared behind a wall that is solid of cursed white. I possibly could only imagine her frantically digging through it and the noise of what was above coming down upon her body. I tried to dig into it myself in search of her body but the layer that remained was frozen solid. It had been like digging my arms into cement and I also knew that Susan could not have survived it, whether or not my mind would not desire to think it during the time. I came across myself picking though I had nothing kept doing at it with tools anyway, experiencing because. I don't know just how much We cried while working at that task that is pointless I do know it started to freeze to my cheeks. I did not stop until my arms could not lift again and that is when I sat among the snow and stared at exactly what my world had become.

I lost track of just how very long I sat there or when I decided to come back towards the fire. I remember once I started burning the Christmas gifts and exactly how hard a choice that had been. I started each one of these gradually and savored the notion of the children playing along with it for the time that is first. I may even see Susan standing over them with her camera in hand. She will be giving her smile that is biggest and snapping away to truly save each memory. She loved pictures that are taking what I had to do did not must be captured on any kind of movie. We started to have the numbness that night, that numbness that is same overtook Susan earlier that day. It had been as cool as the snow that surrounded me and all i really could think was this had been my fault. I will have escaped with my family when I still had the chance. I do not know if it had been pride, ignorance, or both nevertheless the guilt was too much. It ingested me and took away everything this holiday had been supposed to be about.

www.ingramcontent.com/pod-product-compliance
Lightning Source LLC
Chambersburg PA
CBHW052257150726
48001CB00024B/1377